CW01237300

Tragedy at Three Hundred Fathoms
by
Tom Gaston Lt. USN (Ret)

Table of Contents

Introduction 1
Part One: Fate of USS (Redacted) 11
   SitRep 1-The Crew 12
   SitRep 2-Spec Ops Mission 53
   SitRep 3-Fate Plays a Part 110
Part Two: Story of Survival 125
   SitRep 4-Survival 126
   SitRep 5-To be Endured 166
Part Three: Search and Rescue 177
   SitRep 6-SUBMISS/Search 178
   SitRep 7-SUBSUNK/Rescue 191
Part Four: Above and Beyond 219
   SitRep 8-Common Virtue/Uncommon Valor 220
In Memoriam 250
Epilogue 251
Author Biography 252

Copyright © 2021 Tom Gaston

All rights reserved.

ISBN: 979-875-613-976-1

All the characters in this book are fictitious, and any resemblance to actual persons, living or dead, is purely coincidental.

"Dedicated to the brotherhood of men who go down into the seas in boats and wear the coveted Dolphins insignia."

"With special recognition of

"*the Children*" and wives of the men aboard USS Thresher (SSN-593) lost on 10 April 1963 and USS Scorpion (SSN-589) lost on 22 May 1968.

My thoughts and prayers are always with my shipmate and best friend forever… on Eternal Patrol:

Douglas Ray McClelland EM2 (SS) crewmember

USS Thresher (SSN-593)

Forward

"After decades their story and the truth can now be told."

Following the successful completion of extended special operation missions in both the Mediterranean and Black Sea during the period 6 May 1967 through 6 January 1968, the submarine USS (*Redacted)* (SSN-**Hull Number Classified Secret**) was reported missing. After an exhaustive search by surface ships and aircraft, the submarine was located on 24 March 1968 just north of the Canary Islands at the base of an uncharted submerged mountain range at a depth of 300 fathoms beneath the sea. Attempts to salvage and raise the submarine by both the United States Navy and later by the Soviet Military Maritime Fleet failed. Reports of survivors aboard the stricken submarine were never confirmed. In May 1968 the submarine USS *(Redacted)* (SSN-*Hull Number Classified Secret*) was removed from rolls of commissioned U.S. Navy vessels and listed as missing and declared sunk. The official details surrounding the tragic loss of the submarine and its crew were never disclosed and remained classified …until now.

"A work of fiction inspired by many actual events."

Introduction

History of USS *(Redacted)* (SSN-*Hull Number Classified Secret)*

USS *(Redacted)* (SSN-Hull Number Classified Secret) was one of the first boats of her class of nuclear-powered attack submarines. *(Redacted)* construction began on in late April 1957 by the Electric Boat Division of the General Dynamics Corporation in Groton, Connecticut. She was launched on 26 May 1958 and commissioned on 15 April 1960 with Commander R. J Higgins in command.

On the (*Redacted),* there were many design changes that were the results of new engineering efforts into submarine construction and design. The submarine construction industry, with the addition of nuclear power, wanted to make a true submarine. The effort required a unique design in its natural element underwater, one able to remain submerged indefinitely. The greatest change was the tear-dropped shaped hull, included in an earlier design of the conventional diesel powered *Dolphin* class submarine, The *Dolphin* was designed for optimum performance while submerged. The new hull's only protrusions were the sail and diving planes. The sail, very similar to a shark's dorsal fin, rose at a point midway in the hull assisted in maintaining the boat stable. The diving planes, similar in operation to the wings of an airplane, were relocated from the hull to the new redesigned sail, along with the periscopes and antenna masts. They, therefore, could only function when the submarine was submerged like the control surfaces on an aircraft. Also, a single propeller and shaft which would propel (*Redacted*), made it more maneuverable than the traditional twin screw submarine.

The *(Redacted)* nuclear reactor was a Westinghouse S5W and a vast improvement when compared to the USS *Nautilus* reactor allowing the submarine to travel at full power for in excess of 100,000 miles Although the reactor was 30 percent larger than *Nautilus's* reactor, the reactor compartment on *(Redacted)* only occupied 25 feet of the original 252 feet total length. Also, the design of the nuclear reactor core allowed for more accessibility and safety. *(Redacted)* had such advanced underwater capabilities through the water and it could be compared to an airplane in flight.

After her launching in December 1959, *(Redacted)* was the world's fastest submarine after she set the speed record on sea trials in May of the following year. It was designed to have a speed in excess of 20 knots, but its actual speed is a classified. It is estimated that the vessel could have reached approximately 30 knots submerged. This speed was approximately 10 knots faster than the first nuclear submarine *Nautilus* made using the same basic reactor, and essentially equal to the first teardrop shaped submarine *Albacore's* fastest speed submerged.

(Redacted)'s maneuvering capabilities created a whole new outlook with respect to anti-submarine (ASW) problems. She could reverse direction in the distance of her own length, and was referred to as "flying", since *(Redacted)* could climb, dive, and bank like an airplane. During her shakedown cruise in June 1960, she became only the second nuclear submarine to pass through the Straits of Gibraltar and operate in the Mediterranean. Following the post-shakedown period at Groton, Connecticut, she conducted training and participated in advanced Atlantic submarine exercises from August through September 1960, which earned *(Redacted)* a Navy Unit Commendation and a Battle Efficiency "E" award.

In mid-1961, *(Redacted)* entered the channel leading from the Arctic Ocean to Murmansk in the Soviet Union. The details of her voyage remain classified. Upon returning from this mission, *(Redacted)* spent the remainder of 1961 in maintenance upkeep.

(Redacted) commenced her 1962 operations by participating in several weeks of anti-submarine warfare exercises through August and visited Ft. Lauderdale, Florida before returning to Groton. In June 1962, *(Redacted) o*perated out of Key West, Florida, for two weeks before entering the Portsmouth Naval Shipyard in Maine for an extensive overhaul, lasting five months. Following her return to Groton/New London, Connecticut, the submarine operated locally prior to departing in October again for duty in the Mediterranean with the Sixth Fleet. During this deployment, *(Redacted)* participated in NATO exercises and visited Monaco France; and Barcelona Spain, before returning to Groton/New London. In this year, the *(Redacted)* also conducted one of the fastest submerged transits of the Atlantic.

In1963 *(Redacted)* participated in submarine attack operations and ASW exercises, to test the capabilities of the nuclear-powered attack submarine. The highlight of 1963 was two months assignment with NATO forces and visiting Le Havre, France, and the Isle of Portland, England, before returning to Groton/New London in October.

After spending most of 1964 in training exercises, the submarine ended the year by entering the Charleston Naval Shipyard in South Carolina for an overhaul that lasted until October 1964. During this overhaul, preliminary design changes were completed in order to comply with only limited preliminary SUBSAFE certification requirements following the loss of the USS *Thresher* in April 1963. *(Redacted)* then got underway for sea trials off Charleston, before joining *Skipjack* for four days of training near Jacksonville, Florida. *(Redacted)* then was transferred to her new home port of Norfolk, Virginia. She ended the year participating in fleet exercises.

In early in 1965, *(Redacted)* got underway for sonar and weapon tests and then participated in Atlantic submarine exercises from March through June. After which *(Redacted)* participated in training to evaluate ASW aircraft performance against *(Redacted)'s* design characteristics. Following an extended deployment in October and November, the submarine returned to Norfolk to prepare for major operations of that year which she completed early the following year.

In February 1966, *(Redacted)* commenced an extensive early overhaul in the Portsmouth Naval Shipyard which was completed in August 1966. During this overhaul, *(Redacted)* underwent a major hull reconfiguration to incorporate a top-secret experimental twin Newport Rampumpjet (RPJ) propulsion system. The propulsion system incorporated jets on each side of the hull designed to eliminate the underwater cavitation noises associated with the main turbine direct drive single propeller propulsion system. It utilized a steam powered Rampumpjet (RPJ) propulsor by Newport Shipbuilding that combined a shrouded rotor and a stator within a duct to significantly reduce the level of radiated noise and avoid cavitation. It eliminated the need for the conventional cavitating screws to drive the submarine. The hull reconfiguration included a 20 feet extension installed in the auxiliary machinery space to accommodate the Rampumpjet (RPJ) equipment and SUBSAFE design changes. The reconfiguration redirected the topside access hatch from the engine room forward to the auxiliary machinery space. The experimental Rampumpjet (RPJ) during testing could propel the submarine at maximum speed of 12 knots. The steam turbine direct drive single screw would continue to be its main source for propulsion during routine operations. It was anticipated that a future class of submarines would have the RPJ as its primary source of propulsion but would require a substantial advancement in design to reach greater speeds and maneuverability submerged.

During this overhaul, major design changes were also completed in order to comply with final SUBSAFE certification requirements including the main ballast high-pressure air, trim and drain, atmosphere control (O_2 and CO_2) and steam condenser seawater systems. The steam condenser tubes were replaced with enhanced high-grade stainless steel. Duplicate+ systems and equipment were also installed for enhanced safety. These changes included the installation of an emergency high capacity drain pump aft in the engineering compartment and a secondary high capacity carbon dioxide scrubber system with a compressor driven discharge to sea. The enhanced design changes permitted operation of critical systems at deeper depths during emergencies. Many of these early SUBSAFE design changes were later discarded as extreme and unnecessary for implementation in other submarines. The operating depth specifications of the SUBSAFE modifications were classified

After sea trials in September 1966, *(Redacted)* was reassigned to the Naval Station Truman Annex in Key West for extensive testing of the RPJ propulsion system during joint operations with destroyers assigned to the advanced Navy Sonar School based in Key West. The deep depths of the water in and around the Key West operating areas also provided an excellent environment for more extensive testing of the recent SUBSAFE certification design changes.

In early 1967 all scheduled local operations were terminated and she received orders to be deployed to the Mediterranean on special operations.

In May 1968 the submarine USS *(Redacted)* (SSN-*Hull Number Classified Secret*) was removed from rolls of commissioned U.S. Navy vessels and listed as missing and assumed sunk. The details of the fate of the submarine and its crew are unknown and remain classified.

Hull Configuration Diagram of USS *(Redacted)*
(SSN-Hull *Number Classified Secret*)

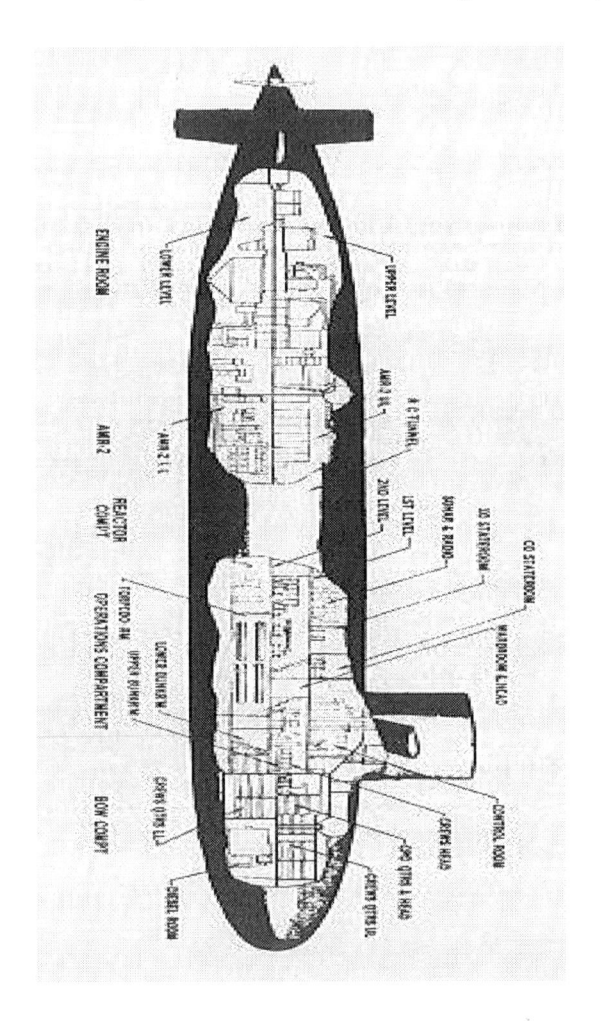

Nuclear USS *(Redacted)* (SSN-Hull *Number Classified Secret)*
Reactor Propulsion System Illustration

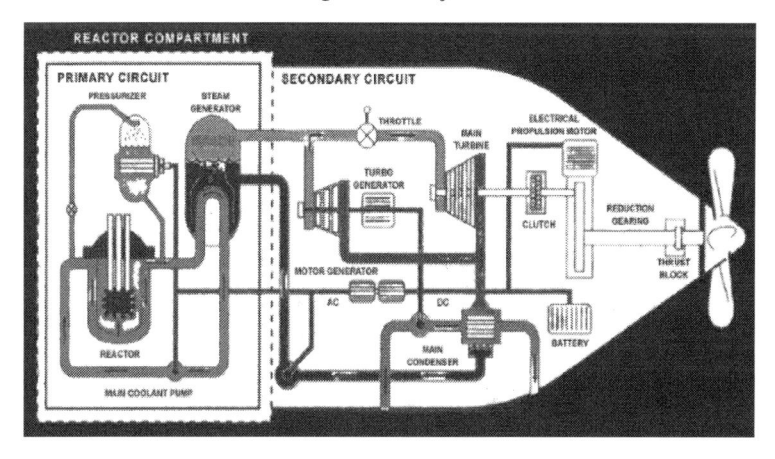

Deep Sea Rescue Vessels (DSRV)

After the loss of the USS *Thresher* several years earlier with all hands aboard, the Navy took actions to ensure such a tragedy as this could never occur again. Following the recommendations of a special Deep Submergence Review Group, the Deep Submergence Rescue System was developed in the late-1960s.

The DSRVs was designed to provide for the rescue of the crew of a submarine sunk on the ocean floor. The submersibles could be transported by land or sea. It can operate independently of surface conditions or under ice for rapid response to an accident anywhere in the world.

The mission of the DSRV is to provide an immediate reaction, worldwide, all weather capability to rescue personnel from disabled submarines at depths of less than 2,000 feet. The DSRVs maximum operating depth is about 4,000 feet and can be transported by truck, aircraft, surface ship, or on a submarine. The DSRV can dive, locate the disabled submarine and attach itself to the sub's rescue seat. After the DSRV is attached to the submarine, the sub's access hatches are opened, and submarine personnel can enter directly into the DSRV. The DSRV then detaches itself from the submarine and delivers the personnel to the support ship. The center and aft compartments accommodate up to 24 passengers and three crewmen.

Under the DSRVs center sphere is a skirt and shock mitigation system that allows the DSRV to mate with the rescue seat on the submarine's escape trunk or access hatch. The skirt allows a watertight seal to be made between the DSRV and the submarine. After a seal is made, the submarine's upper access hatch can be opened and swung up into the skirt cavity.

Propulsion and control of the DSRV is provided by a conventional battery and four propellers, two forward and two aft. The system permits the DSRV to maneuver and hover in underwater currents. The DSRV can attach to a submarine inclined to angles up to 45 degrees from vertical in both the fore and aft or athwart ships direction, and in a current of up to two knots.

In early 1960, the Soviet Union in response to the loss of several submarines and crews significantly increased the funding and development of the DSRV. By 1966 they had completed the construction and testing of two advanced DSRVs capable of rescue operations at depths greater than 2,000 feet.

References:
1. Some excerpts and data from Wikipedia the free encyclopedia
2. Naval Ships Diagram of hull configuration does not include Rampumpjet modifications.
3. Also incorporates some text from the public domain. Dictionary of American Naval Fighting Ships.

Part One: Fate of USS (Redacted)

SitRep 1-The Crew

The silence was suddenly broken by a blast of noise… followed by a gust of air… a wall of green and then darkness… nothing but peaceful darkness. Through the labyrinth of darkness flashes of light spiraled past becoming faster and faster and then stopped with a crack as suddenly as it began.

The sun reflected off the small white rocks along the blacktop road. An occasional small seashell added a variety of color to the surroundings. The palm trees swayed slightly in the gentle sea breeze but were sometimes difficult to see in the glaring sun. To the right there were white buildings used as warehouses and to the left… the ocean. The water was calm and an unexpected light green with only patches of blue. Small waves of white foam formed in the distance and then died likes ripples in a pond as they reached the sands of the long narrow rocky beach.

A tall dark-haired man walked down the road. His dark blue Navy uniform contrasted sharply with the bright surroundings. His round Navy white hat was pushed to the back of his head. On his uniform he wore his many service ribbons as well as silver metal pin of a submarine flanked by two dolphins. The Dolphins are the insignia of the submarine force. He carried his sea bag over his shoulder. The green duffel bag containing all of his belongings, were packed tight and neat for his next duty station. The effect of the heavy load and the heat was evident by the streams of sweat pouring down his face. The moisture caused his clothing to cling to his body. He itched but couldn't scratch. He was tired but couldn't rest. His destination, only a few hundred yards away, seemed miles away. *"A cold beer, he thought. Give my nuts for just one cold beer. Damn! It's hot! Wish I had changed out these dress blues to my tropical whites before heading south. No damn snow ever falls here that's for sure."*

At one of the many docking piers, two submarines swayed in opposite directions and strained against their mooring lines located fore and aft. Waves from a passing ship splashed against the sides of the subs driving them against the pier and one another. The coral covered pilings weaken by rot, cracked from the impact. On the decks men in their dungaree work uniforms were busy loading crates. Some were painting while others just lay in the sun, most without shirts or hats.

The exhausted sailor carried his bag across the gangway of the first boat to the second, saluted the flag flying from the stern and addressed the topside watch on duty.

"Reporting aboard for duty."

"Name, rate and serial number?" The watch asked. "I also need your orders."

"Corbett, James C. Electrician's Mate First Class, 466-44-82."

"Very well," the watch replied as he entered his name into the ship's deck log.

The watch proceeded to the raised superstructure of the submarine, picked up a microphone and called. "Below decks… topside."

"Below Decks!" a voice returned over the speaker.

"Man reporting aboard," the watch replied.

After a pause the voice from below answered. "Send him below and I'll escort him to the duty officer. Next time keep your mouth back from the microphone and you don't have to yell. I'm not deaf you non-qual dip shit."

"Topside watch, aye," the young sailor returned and added, "Fuckin hard ass," only after making quite sure the microphone was off.

"My name is Snell; welcome aboard. I've been aboard about six months. It's a good boat I'm sure that you will like it," he said in rapid but nervous succession. "You can leave your sea bag here with me until you get assigned a bunk and locker. I have to hot bunk it with a couple of guys. I'm sure you will get your own bunk since you are qualified and first class. We have a full crew. Lots of extra guys on board. Probably for our next deployment. Haven't told us much about it yet."

Corbett replied, "Right. That sucks! Thanks Snell. I'm sure I will like it, or I will manage. They always tell us what we need to know when we need to know, I guess. Make sure you keep an eye on my shit. See you later," as he turned and walked to the access hatch leading below decks. Stopping at the hatch, he asked, "That below decks watch was kinda rough on you Snell for no reason. You behind on your quals by chance?"

"Yeah, I guess you could say that."

"You need any help learning a system or a walk through, maybe I can give you a hand," Corbett suggested. "You have to speak up sometimes when you are having trouble, or everyone will just think you are lazy and a slacker."

"Thanks. I will do that. I only have three more months to finish my qual card or I'm going to be in deep shit," the young sailor replied with a half-smile.

"Just stay focused on the prize sailor and you will do well," Corbett remarked as he continued down the access hatch below.

Seaman First Class Snell is a designated sonarman. He reported aboard after Class A trade school and hopes to make petty officer third class on the next exam. You can tell he is from Massachusetts by his strong accent. He is single with a girl back home and another locally in town. He will have to work hard to learn the systems aboard his submarine. After completing his qualification card signed by experienced qualified operators on each system, he will get a walk through the boat by his leading petty officer and then the operations officer. He'll get his Dolphins, (insignia of the submarine services) after passing a final written exam and then an oral exam by a board of three senior crew members.

Corbett climbed down the ladder of the long, black, teardrop shaped submarine and had descended about ten feet when he reached the first level of the bow compartment. The below decks watch met him to escort him aft to the Duty Officer's stateroom in the operations compartment.

He was amazed at the enormous array of equipment in the modern nuclear-powered submarine although it was quite similar to the other nuclear-powered submarines which he had served aboard for his previous eight years in the Navy. He had served on the sister ship of *(Redacted)*. He stopped momentarily in the passageway. Something on a nearby bulkhead caught his eye. It was the centerfold of the latest issue of *Playboy* magazine. "Fantastic," he remarked with a sigh as he stopped and studied the picture at length.

The watch turned in search of Corbett, whom he thought was directly behind him. "Make it snappy, Sailor. The duty officer is waiting," he said with a disgusted tone to his voice.

"Keep your shirt on, Mate. You have to establish priorities in your life, or you'll never get anywhere," Corbett replied with a smile as he continued after him.

The watch smiled for the first time as he said, "Yes, I see what you mean."

The two men stopped in front of a stateroom and the watch knocked. "Sir, this is Petty Officer Corbett, new man reporting aboard."

"Come in. My name is Lieutenant Eddy," the officer said as he stood up from his desk and shook Corbett's hand. "I'm the engineering officer. Since you're an electrician, I will be your department head. I see from your service record that you are a qualified reactor operator and the propulsion plant as well as engineering officer of the watch (EOW). I am very impressed. I am sure you will learn our power plant very quickly and help with the newer non-quals."

"Thank you, Sir. It's good to be aboard," Corbett replied with a grin.

Lieutenant John Eddy is a short, stocky man. He has a ruddy red face and bald except for a patch of hair on each side, cut very short. His eyes were bloodshot from an obvious lack of sleep and the neglect of a pair of eyeglasses gathering dust sitting alongside his smoldering pipe. He is what is commonly called a mustang. He had advanced from the enlisted ranks and earned his commission nine years ago when he was a chief petty officer. The strain of his many responsibilities has made him old before his time. The workday starts early and finishes even later. A sixty-hour week was considered a vacation. He has to keep the engineering plant of a modern submarine running with little or no administrative help, a shortage of experienced personnel and a shortage of funds in a peace-time Navy. He was rejected twice by Admiral Rickover before being accepted to attend Commissioned Officer Nuclear Power and Submarine School. He has an additional year to serve as a commissioned officer before he can request retirement.

Admiral Hyman J. Rickover is known as the father of the nuclear submarine. As a captain assigned to the Bureau of Ships, he had a plan to install a small nuclear reactor into a submarine. The nuclear reactor would allow the submarine to stay submerged indefinitely without the need for outside air required for the operation of traditional diesel submarines. Rickover took his idea (without the approval of the Bureau of Ships) to Electric Boat Shipbuilding. Electric Boat developed the design in the hope of getting a contract which he then presented to the Bureau of Ships. The project for the first nuclear submarine USS *Nautilus* was immediately approved for construction. He is known to be a tough, no nonsense, hard ass and obviously intelligent officer. He controls the nuclear submarine force with an iron fist and will (without hesitation or discussion) relieve any commanding officer or junior officer with the slightest infraction and send them packing to other duties.

Lieutenant Eddy stood up from his chair. Putting on his hat he said, "You'll get your belly full of sea duty on the (**Redacted**). We are known to be underway more than we are in port except for refitting and overhauls and it doesn't look like it's going to get any better in the near future," the stocky man remarked with a sigh. "You'll find the duty chief petty officer below in the crew's quarters. He'll assign you a bunk for tonight and you'll probably meet the captain and the executive officer tomorrow."

"Thank you, Sir," Corbett replied and asked, "What are our operations coming up?"

"We get underway in the morning for spec ops. It's an intelligence mission, classified secret so keep that fact under your hat. That's all I can tell you now. I have to make my rounds below decks."

"Aye, aye, Sir," Corbett replied as he left the stateroom and proceeded aft and below to the crew's quarters.

"This is your bunk, Corbett," the chief petty officer said. "You have liberty today. Quarters are at 0800 in the morning. My name is Sneed, Chief Torpedoman," he added, shaking Corbett's hand.

"Thanks, Chief."

"Your Leading Petty Officer (LPO) is Chief Sullivan. You'll meet him tomorrow."

"What kind of guy is he?" Corbett asked.

"Good man. He works hard and plays hard. He'll go to bat for you and back you all the way, but never cross him," the chief said convincingly.

"Thanks, I'll remember that," Corbett returned.

The Chief returned to the crew's mess hall to catch the scheduled afternoon movie as Corbett spent the day getting acquainted with the rest of his new home. He was shown all three levels of the operations compartment, the reactor compartment, the auxiliary machinery space, and, finally, the engine room including the maneuvering room located in the stern. He also met some of the 12 officers and 99 enlisted men aboard who were to be his shipmates for the next year.

Corbett learned that Chief Torpedoman Jack Sneed is a very intelligent but unhappy person. His wife forced him to make a choice between her and the Navy. He chose the Navy and regretted it afterwards. He seldom leaves the boat. On board, he seldom leaves the bow compartment where the torpedoes are stowed. His hobby is guns and he is responsible for the ship's armory. His eyelashes, eyebrows and most of his hair were recently burned away in an accident with black powder.

Second Class Commissaryman Rodger "Red" Thomas is the best ship's cook in the area. He wears his red, curly hair rather long. His body is covered with tattoos, including two flies on the foreskin of his penis. He loves to drink almost as much as he loves to fight. Each time Red is promoted to chief petty officer, he soon manages to get busted back to petty officer third class. One incident occurred as he was returning to his boat one-night drunk, after a night on the town. He was confronted by two Marine sentries at the main gate in such a manner that was totally to his disliking. A left to the mid-section and a right cross sent one of the Marines sprawling to the gutter. He decked the second with a knee to the groin and proceeded to urinate in his face while holding him at bay with his own forty-five caliber pistol. The second reduction in rate was a small punishment considering the offense. The supply officer discovered that Red was serving ship's stores in his privately owned restaurant in town. Many people wondered why he could be allowed to remain in the Navy, much less the Submarine Service. A good cook, however, is an asset to the moral of the crew and cherished by many commanding officers. He along with two other Commissaryman and three mess cooks prepare the meals for the crew of 111 men aboard *(Redacted)*.

Seaman Apprentice Barry Barns, called Beebe, is 17 years old and reported aboard two months prior. He is assigned temporary duty as a mess cook in the crew's mess. He along with two other mess cooks assist Petty Officer Thomas in the more menial tasks associated with the preparation of food for the crew. His duty as mess cook is scheduled to last 6 months and he will likely serve again before he is promoted to the rank of petty officer third class. He was not selected to attend a technical (Class A) school immediately out of boot camp and has not decided which specialty or rate he wants to learn through on-board training. He did request, was selected and graduated from the Enlisted Naval Submarine School located at Groton/New London, Connecticut. As a mess cook, his workday starts at 0500 in the morning and often ends at 2200 at night. His lack of standing or status as a low ranking non-qualified newbie among the crew is often demonstrated by the attitude and actions of his shipmates. On one occasion Seaman Apprentice Barns proceeded topside through the forward access hatch. He was carrying two trash cans, commonly referred to as shit cans, from the crew's mess to the pier for dumping. He was walking toward the gangway leading to the dumpster on the pier when he tripped over his long white apron and, along with the shit cans, fell over the curved side of the boat into the water between the pier and boat. The water below was covered with a collection of nasty fuel oil and miscellaneous trash. He believes that he hit his head on the side of the boat and swallowed some of the accumulated fuel oil which rendered him almost unconscious. The boat, along with Seaman Apprentice Barns, dangerously swayed back and forth against the rotting pilings of the pier pushed by the harbor waves. As he fell, he vividly recalls hearing a crew member topside yelling out, "Save the shit cans... save the shit cans." The shit cans are made of stainless steel and, obviously unlike Seaman Apprentice Barns, very expensive to replace.

Third Class Interior Communications Technician Donald Ellsworth (Elvis) is from California. He continuously brags about his conquest of the opposite sex. He is often called "trench mouth" because his vocabulary consists mostly of four-letter words. He dislikes the Navy and is often referred to as a short timer with a short timer's attitude. He carries a short timer's chain on his belt and removes a link of chain each week to mark his time left. He did graduate first in his class from Navy Nuclear Power School, qualified in submarines and received his Dolphins in record time. He has the potential to do very well in the Navy if he decides to reenlist which is not likely.

Sonar Technician Third Class Robert Robishaw Esquire III is from New York. He is commonly called Robby or Robin Hood since he often brags about his English ancestry. His family is said to be financially well off and had disowned their only son for his bad behavior as well as dropping out of Hartford University six months before graduation. He never wants to talk much about his reasons for joining the Navy, but some say that it has something to do with an engagement that went wrong. Surprisingly he has a case of claustrophobia which he manages to keep under control. The claustrophobia was caused by an accident he had during submarine escape training while in submarine school. All potential submariners must successfully complete an escape from a depth of 100 feet. The training escape is made from a tank 100 feet high filled with water. The submarine school student enters a compartment at the base of the escape training tank. The compartment is pressurized to 44 psi which equalizes with the pressure at a depth of 100 feet in the tank. The submarine school student then enters at the bottom of the tank and ascends to the top exhaling all the way up. Robishaw was unable to equalize his right ear as the pressure increased in the escape entrance compartment. He experienced severe pain in his ear as the pressure was increased before he entered the tank and then decreased as he ascended to the top. He was able to endure the pain as he made his escape. He did not want to be disqualified and kicked out of submarine school, so he said nothing about his eardrum injury. His injury healed without much difficulty. A lasting effect, however, is panic when he enters a closed in area. He can keep his anxiety to a minimum aboard his submarine and performs all his assigned duties.

The submarine escape training accomplished by all submarine school students is an outdated requirement. It was developed for WWII conventional submarines. Modern nuclear submarines, such as (***Redacted***), operate at much deeper depths and are unlikely to be stranded in shallow water of 100 or even 300 feet. It does, however, weed out the weak minded and less dedicated sailors who volunteer for submarines. It quickly turns mama's boy into a man.

Electronics Technician First Class Ted Franklin, nicknamed Francis, has a year of college paid for by the Navy and has attended just about every school in his field. His current six-year enlistment is over in nine months. He has a guaranteed job with a major electronics firm waiting for him at a salary of $20,000 a year. He is referred to as a slick arm first class since he made his rank before adding a four-year hash mark on the sleeve of his uniform. He often jokingly criticizes the service. He does realize, however, how lucky he is. When he enlisted in the Navy, he was a high school dropout pumping gas in a service station. He was engaged and planned to be married in a few days. He quickly left his hometown of El Paso, Texas and joined the Navy when he discovered that his fiancée was not pregnant as he was led to believe.

Hospital Corpsman First Class (Doc) Samuel Kline is very well liked by the entire crew. He has been married many times. The number changes with every sea story he tells. He was only recently released from the base hospital. After drinking a fifth of tequila and chasing it with elderberry wine, he was arrested naked in a phone booth along Ocean Parkway attempting to make a collect telephone call to the POTUS. For many days, Sam honestly believed that he was the ambassador from England and had just swum the Atlantic Ocean. He vowed never to drink again.

Quartermaster Second Class James (Jim) Rankin has been in the Navy for 10 years. He is married to a local girl of Cuban decent and has two children. His wife is expecting a third in several months. He is glad to be stationed in his wife's adopted hometown of Key West again since her large family is a good support group. He met his wife to be while on weekend liberty in Havana, Cuba before the rise of Castro and helped her immigrate to Key West to join much of her family. At that time, he was serving aboard the USS *Sennet* (SS408) in Key West which soon changed its homeport to Charleston. His family has accumulated a lot of debt to finance the many moves from duty station to duty station over the years. Moving his family is very expense and the Navy pays very little to cover the actual expenses. He passed the last three advancement exams for first class petty officer but was not promoted since there are far too many first-class quartermasters in the Navy. He can't support his family on Navy pay and draws welfare. He is considering not reenlisting after his current tour of duty is over, but he doesn't see many opportunities as a civilian with experience as a quartermaster in the Navy. Along with two other quartermasters he assists the navigator who is responsible for the safe position of the submarine at all times. The hazards of the sea on the surface or below are many.

Machinist's Mate First Class Donald White is married with one child. He also pays child support for an illegitimate child in his hometown of Pascagoula, Mississippi. His wife works to help with the family budget. He is an easy-going guy and goes out of his way to get along with his fellow shipmates. He finished last in his class at the Navy Nuclear Power School in Groton/New London, Connecticut. He qualified and received his Dolphins in record time since everyone was willing to go out of their way to help him. His job is to operate and maintain the steam turbines and associated equipment in the boat's engine room.

Seaman Walt (Wally) Wallace has been in the service for nine months. He joined the Navy to avoid the draft. He is more than willing to put in the many hours and work hard to earn his silver Dolphins. He is referred to as the Professor because of his obsession with perfection. He knows well that the symbol of the Submarine Service could only be worn after learning the many complicated systems aboard his submarine. He wants to be an electronic technician which is a difficult field to learn and make third class petty officer since he had not attended the specialized Navy trade school before Submarine School.

Electrician's Mate Third Class Michael Lee is the quiet type and a loner. He is intelligent but has not performed at his full potential. He has acquired many debts which he cannot or will not pay. He received several warnings at Commanding Officer's Non-Judicial Punishment for his debts as well as fighting. Very few people like him, and he is avoided by the crew as much as possible. He is consistently behind on his systems qualification schedule and assigned extra duty by his leading petty officer (LPO).

The newest member of the crew, Electrician's Mate First Class James Corbett, joined the Navy after graduating from high school. Like most men in the service, he has a girl back home but is uncertain if he is ready for marriage. He joined the Navy to see the world and has a very good start on his goal. He has a short temper inherited from his father's Indian blood. He is intelligent and was recently selected as an alternate for the Navy's Enlisted Scientific Education Program. After earning his bachelor's degree at a university of his choice, he will receive his commission as an officer. He is first required to complete his tour of one year of temporary duty aboard *(Redacted)* before going to college with full pay and allowances. As an enlisted non-commissioned officer, he was the first person of his rank as petty officer second class to qualify as engineering officer of watch (EOW). This responsibility is normally assigned to chief petty officers or commissioned officers. He is qualified to operate and supervise all engineering positions including the nuclear reactor as well as responding to all emergency situations. He served as an instructor at the land based S1W prototype reactor located at the Idaho National Engineering Laboratory near Arco, Idaho. The plant is the prototype for the power system of USS *Nautilus* (SSN-571). He trained many sailors in the operation and maintenance of submarine nuclear power plants following their graduation from Navy Nuclear Power school and before their assignment to a nuclear submarine. He trained and knew personally many of the crew of the USS *Thresher* (SSN 593) which sank on 10 April 1963 with all hands. As with many submarine sailors, the loss of USS *Thresher* affected him very deeply.

These are only a few of the 99 enlisted men of the crew of *(Redacted.)* They are unconventional, but real people, described in unconventional terms. Conventionally, they are men with likes and dislikes, good traits and bad traits, successes and failures; forced together in an atmosphere of mutual trust; a trust necessary to function where each man's life depends upon the decisions and actions of the other. The unreliable are weeded out and disposed of in a ritual of acceptance which is unwritten, but constantly proven by the boredom of the day to day routine, long term isolation and the unexpected.

Corbett and White emerged from the aft access hatch and stood on deck talking for a few moments.

The sun had set, and the night air was cool. The sky was clear, but smelled damp as if it were about to rain. The bright, mooring lights of the larger ships at the nearby piers blended with the stars high in the sky. Music from someone's portable radio could be heard playing in the distance.

A few sailors were fishing from the pier at the stern of the submarine. The inboard diesel submarine suddenly started its main engines in preparation for its routine charge of the boat's batteries before getting underway the following morning. The overboard saltwater discharge sprayed across the pier wetting down the unsuspecting sailors. They scurried in all directions cursing and laughing.

"Are you going on liberty?" White asked.

"Yeah, I thought I'd go into town for a couple of drinks and terrorize the local natives a bit."

White laughed. "I'm afraid there's not much happening over there. It's pretty dead, even on a Saturday night."

"If there's something loose, I'll find it."

"I bet you will," White returned. "If I didn't have the duty and wasn't married, I'd like to go with you."

"Glad to have you anytime. I want to thank you for showing me through the boat."

"Think nothing of it… my pleasure. I know how it is being a new man onboard. If the guys give you the silent treatment for a few days, don't worry about it. It's just a standard joke they play on all new men."

"Thanks for warning me. That could drive you up a tree. I'll see you later, and thanks again," he added as he crossed the gangway and headed up the pier.

Corbett's second trip on the blacktopped road in the cool night air was much more pleasant than the first. He had changed from his dress blue uniform to his more comfortable whites. He quickly made his way out the main gate of the Naval Base into the nearby town.

The city, like many Navy supported communities, is abundant with bars and people who dislike sailors. Being in a tropical climate, it is noted for its fishing and mosquitoes. It is well known that if you are ever unlucky enough to be stranded in the Keys leading south from Miami at night you were in danger from the large mosquitoes that swarm in great numbers. The few tourists who make it to the city realize their mistake and quickly depart.

Corbett was still making the rounds of the drinking establishments on Duval Street when he entered Sloppy Joe's and sat down at the bar. The waitress behind the bar caught his attention right away. She appeared to be in her early twenties but could have been older. She is, what most would consider to be, very attractive. She is tall and with dark hair down to her waist. As she walked toward him, she had a smile which was an obvious message that Corbett recognized and picked up right away. With that smile, she glanced at him, lowered her head slightly before looking away and then forced to look back again.

She approached and asked, "What'll it be, Sailor?"

"Rum and Coke, please," he replied.

"Okay, I'll add a twist of lime and make it a Cuba Libre for good measure," she returned.

"Anything you say. You're the expert."

She returned shortly with his drink, took his money and gave him his change minus a substantial tip.

"What time do you get off work?" he asked.

"One AM," she replied as she cleaned the bar in front of him. It was merely an excuse to stay and talk rather than serve other waiting thirsty customers.

Corbet took her hand and held it lightly and said with his best smile, "I'm in need of some… deep and I do mean deep…conversation with a member of the opposite sex. How about it? I'll even fix breakfast for you when we wake up."

"You're fast on your feet. Guys usually wait a few hours before they pop the question," she said with a vigorous laugh.

"I have to be fast. I talk slow," he whispered as he held his lips to the back of her hand which emitted a tantalizing fragrance. "Would you like to dance?" he added.

"Sorry. Not allowed to fraternize with the customers," she replied as she placed her other hand on top of his and stroked it ever so gently. She was shifting her weight for one foot to other while resting against the bar in front of him and was obviously more than a little aroused. She picked up his other hand, placed a finger to her lips, kissed it before placing the tip gently in her mouth. She abruptly realized things were going a little too far.

"I like your style. Meet me outside at one o'clock," she remarked with that same smile as she reluctantly retrieved her hand and walked away.

He noticed the shape of her short leather skirt from behind and took a long deep breath. "I'll be waiting."

He sat sipping his drink as he looked around the dimly lit bar. It was crowded with sailors, talking loudly and drinking heavily. A couple was dancing with slow gyrating hips near the juke box without music. Directly across at the end of the half-moon shaped bar, a sailor sat with his head resting on his arm on the bar. He was obviously drunk. Corbett looked again and recognized Sam (Doc) Kline. "How in the hell did he get that drunk so fast?" he whispered to himself as he shook his head with a curious smile.

Two Canadian Sailors entered the bar. The only two empty seats were on either side of Corbett. The taller and huskier of the two stood behind Corbet, lifted him from his seat by the underarms and placed him one seat to the left and remarked, "Thanks, Mate, mighty nice of you," as the two sat side by side at the bar.

"What the hell?" Corbet remarked as he grabbed his bar stool to keep from falling. After reconsidering his first impulse to just deck his ass, Corbett thought for a second and replied with a smirk, "Not at all. Limeys are noted for their courtesy. Tell me you stupid asshole. You fuck the Queen lately or does she prefer to just suck your dick? If you don't like that Mate, just eat shit and die motherfucker." All this time, he continued to sip his drink and look straight ahead. His use of such extreme profanity came as a complete surprise and shock to him but decided it was a necessary and appropriate response.

Canadians do not like to be associated in any way with their counterparts in the English Navy referred to as Limeys. To say the least, they consider it to be an insult. They do, however, love and respect her Majesty the Queen of England. The mother reference did not sit well at all either. With no advanced warning, the husky Canadian looked to one side at Corbett with a grimace and came back quickly with his left elbow catching Corbett square in the mouth. The blow sent Corbett tumbling backwards from his bar stool to the floor with a thud. Without even looking around, the two sailors continued their conversation obviously thinking the confrontation was over.

The bar suddenly became quiet.

Shaking his head and dusting off his trousers, Corbett stood up, cupped his hands together and from behind dealt the husky sailor a heavy, double-handed blow to his right kidney. The sailor fell from the bar stool to the floor in agony. The second sailor quickly retaliated with a beer bottle to Corbett's head, driving him back against the jukebox. Shattered glass covered the floor as sailors crouched for cover. Many people hurried out the door while others just stood and watched.

The two men met in a frenzy of blows in the middle of the room which sent both men slamming to the floor. As they stood up entangled, a quick hard left to the stomach and a follow through rabbit punch to the back of the neck by Corbett sent the Canadian slamming back to the floor, half unconscious. The husky sailor was attempting to get to his feet when Corbett landed a solid kick to the side of his head. Both Canadians were on the floor done.

Corbett quickly grabbed his white hat from the bar and exited from the rear door as a squad of shore patrol entered through the front. He hurried down the back alley, up a side street and lost himself in the sparse crowd back on Duval Street.

He entered the nearest, darkest bar and went straight to the head commonly referred to by civilians as the men's room. Only then did he begin to feel his aches and pains. He noticed the large bump on his forehead. It was painful to the touch and smeared with blood. He tasted blood from a cut on his lip and his side throbbed with pain. He doused his face with water and muttered, "Damn Canucks, no sense of humor."

As he looked around the bar, it was very dark and almost empty except for a few men in civilian clothes. The place had a ripe, sweet but foul smell which caused him to think for moment that he should leave. With his lingering aches and pains, he decided that trying to walk very far was not a good idea. He sat down and noticed what appeared to be a female sitting at the end of the bar. He wasn't sure of the gender. She smiled but he could not care less since he was not the least bit interested in starting a conversation. Two men were sitting in a booth across the room and to his left. He noticed that one man had his arm around the neck of the other while whispering in his ear and kissing his cheek. "Oh well," he mumbled to himself. "Not my cup of tea but to each his own."

Corbett sat at the bar and drank more than a few rum and Coke. It was almost one o'clock when the bartender announced last call for alcohol before closing. Corbett had a decision to make and pondered the alternatives. Quarters for muster were at 0800 and the boat was due to get underway at 0900. In a few hours he would face a full day's work and shuttered at the thought of how he would feel. He knew he should return to his boat and get some sleep, but thoughts of the tall brunette persisted in his mind. He made the only decision possible as he left the bar and proceeded in the direction of Sloppy Joe's.

He stood hidden in a doorway next to the bar, observing the entrance anxiously awaiting her exit. He didn't have to wait long. The brunette appeared in the doorway. He made a motion toward her but quickly stopped and retreated for a second glance. The husky Canadian he had confronted earlier came out of the bar and entangled her waist with his arm. She giggled at one of his remarks as they quickly paced off in the opposite direction, her short skirt riding even higher on her hips, encouraged by the sailor's left hand. Corbett could only stand and watch as they disappeared down the dimly lit deserted street. He turned, put his hands in the waist band of his trousers and walked slowly in the direction of the base.

Like an exquisite pheasant in flight from the hunter's gun, a trout from the fisherman's line, the beautiful prey was gone. The despondent hunter must go hungry again tonight.

Onboard (**Redacted**) in the crew's quarters, Corbett removed his uniform and placed it in his locker. Dressed only in his Navy issue white skivvies, black socks and tee shirt, he grasped an overhanging pipe and raised himself to the middle bunk of a triple rack. "Damn broad," he mumbled. "I can't say much for her taste in men," as he drifted off to sleep.

"She was on the bed. The light reflected off her naked body. He lowered himself and embraced her slowly. The feeling of warmth, softness and enchantment caused first a tingle then a flood of ecstasy which started in his groin and spread the length of his body."

Corbett rose quickly, hitting his head on the upper bunk. Lying back in his pillow, he could hear the whirling noise of running machinery in the distance and the sound of snoring in the darkness. The smell of amine from the carbon dioxide scrubbers, fuel oil and unwashed feet penetrated his nostrils. Faint outlines of the people sleeping around him slowly materialized from the darkness. The feeling of wetness became evident as he turned to his side.

"Damn broad," he muttered as he tried to sleep, hoping to continue his dream. His thoughts continued to wander. *"A dream lasts only a few seconds. A few seconds lived and never to be relived. Gone...it's gone. What is a dream? What is reality? They are experiences. Experiences of dreams and reality merged in the depths of memory are indistinguishable except by reason. I must remember to write that down,"* he thought. He slept without dreaming.

"Reveille... Reveille! Up all hands, clean sweep down fore and aft. Dump all trash and garbage on the pier," suddenly blared over the general announcing system, followed by "First call, first call to breakfast."

Corbett, awakened by the unexpected announcement, sat up quickly, striking his head once again on the bunk above him.

"Damn it!" he shouted, rubbing his swollen head. "I'll kill myself before I'm used to this bunk."

"Up and at'em, Sailors. It's gonna be a bright, sunny day. A great day to go sailing," the below decks watch shouted, passing through the crew's berthing area and turning on the lights. Uproar of insults and four-letter words came from the stirring bunks. A pillow flew across the compartment and struck the watch in the face.

"Is that any way to treat a dedicated, motivated, hard-working individual who is diligently defending his country?" the watch asked with a phony whimper.

"Somebody take that pillow and shove it up his ass. Maybe that'll shut him up," a voice returned.

"Alright you guys," the watch continued. "I'm usually a nice guy but you've made me mad. Now get the hell up or I'll have your ass in a sling." The sailors ignored his order.

Corbett swung down from his bunk, gathered his shaving gear and hurried to the crew's head for a shower. After his shower, he stood in line behind three other sailors for his turn at one of three wash basins. He greeted the sailor next to him but received no response. After shaving, he dressed in his dungaree working uniform, shined his shoes, grabbed his white hat stuffing it in his belt and hurried off in the direction of the crew's mess. He realized that he hadn't eaten anything since the previous morning, and he was famished.

He passed White in the passageway. "It looks like you found something loose alright," White said, "the loose end of a big stick. What happened to your face?"

"Small door... bad eyes, you know," Corbett replied as he went on his way.

The mess hall was almost filled. Some men were dressed in their dress uniforms, having just returned from liberty. Others were in their working uniforms, covered with grease, oil and sweat from a long night's work. The night before getting underway is always a busy time. Equipment had to be repaired, checks made, and material stowed in preparation for going to sea. The largest task to be accomplished is bringing the nuclear reactor up to power, warming up the steam plant and testing the boat's propulsion system.

"What'll it be?" Red asked. "Steak and eggs are the specialty of the house every Sunday morning."

"Steak ...well done and... yeah three eggs... over easy," Corbett replied.

"Right away," the cook replied as he straightened the tall, white chef's hat covering his long, red, curly hair. "Better hope the XO doesn't notice your punch-drunk face. Your ass will be in a sling answering a bunch of questions I am sure you don't want to answer," he continued with a smile. "Check with Doc. He can handle those cuts on your head. Looks like you got on the wrong side of a beer bottle."

"Yes, you are right. Would not care to answer questions unless I have to," Corbett replied. "You should see the other guy."

"You need some help setting things right with this guy, just let me know," Red said with a grin. "Next time we have liberty when we get back, you and I can have a talk with him. One that he will never forget. Based upon that cut on your head, I can tell that he loves to use a damn beer bottle to increase his odds. I hate guys that have to resort to shit like that. Really pisses me off."

Corbett laughed. "Well, there were two guys not just a him. Thanks for the offer though, Red. I really do appreciate it, but those guys are long gone," Corbett replied. "On their way back to Canada I would say."

"Two Canuck sailors?" Red questioned with a smirk. "Damn! Well done Sailor," he said as he continued with his cooking.

As Corbett took his seat in the crew's mess, he had to smile as he thought about the strange but unusually friendly encounter he just had with his new shipmate. He didn't know what to make of it. He knew that they would probably not get to be good friends but appreciated the sincere gesture he had just experienced. He quickly downed the breakfast, drew a second cup of coffee and climbed the access hatch leading topside. He crossed the gangways of the two boats and sat down on one of the pilings of the pier.

The sky to the east was clear and gray, waiting patiently for the sun to make an appearance. Far to the west on the horizon, dark thunder clouds were visible in the fading moon light. Rain was falling from the clouds in light gray sheets, resembling a sheer curtain blowing in the wind. Occasionally, a flash of light would appear, illuminating the sky and obscure horizon, followed by a clap of thunder dying reluctantly like an echo in a mountain canyon.

The deck of the submarine and pier were quickly becoming more populated with sailors talking, drinking coffee, laughing and walking around in anticipation of things to come. A sailor yelled and cursed when he almost fell over the curved side of the sub from a friendly shove by one of his shipmates. Corbett just sat on the piling of the pier, slowly sipping hot coffee. He took a deep breath of the cool morning breeze trying to clear his groggy head.

"You must be Corbett." a voice came from behind. "I'm Burgess... Chief of the Boat."

Corbett stood up, approached the chief and shook his hand. "Yes, COB. That's me," he replied.

Burgess is a Master Chief Machinist Mate with 18 years in the submarine service. He served on the *Nautilus* and was onboard when the boat made its historic transit under the ice cap of the Arctic. He was on the commissioning crew of the George Washington, first Intercontinental Ballistic Missile (ICBM) submarine. He also served aboard two fast attack submarines similar to (***Redacted***). As chief of the boat (COB) and assistant to the executive officer (XO), he has the enormous responsibility for every aspect of the running the day to day operations of the submarine. Every watch station on the boat must be manned by the most qualified men. The crew stands rotating watches with four hours on watch and four off. While not on watch the crew performs duties associated with their job ratings which includes keeping the equipment operating. The many senior leading petty officers were assigned by the COB to supervise these responsibilities in their areas of expertise. The submarine's readiness depends solely upon the training of the crew during all evolutions which he devotes much of his time. He is also responsible to ensure that new crew members became fully qualified to operate all systems aboard the submarine. The exception is the operation of (***Redacted***)**'s** nuclear reactor and associated components in the engineering compartment. These duties are restricted to graduates of the Navy Nuclear Power

School. These restrictions create a division among the crew unlike the crews of the conventional diesel-powered submarines in the fleet. He is acutely aware of this division and the morale problems it often creates.

"Glad to have you aboard. I read your service record," Burgess said. "I see that you qualified on a smoke boat but then re-qualified on Skipjack. Since she is our sister ship, I am sure that you will be able to carry your load quickly. We are short on qualified senior electricians and electronic technicians right now. I see that you are also qualified as reactor operator and EOW. I am counting on you to take up the slack. Help get the young EM strikers and fireman qualified as soon as possible. Your LPO Sullivan can sure use the help. Have you met him yet this morning?"

"Not yet, COB."

"I didn't think so. That's why I wanted to talk to you," he explained. "Your maneuvering watch station is propulsion control in the maneuvering room. Chief Sullivan will be there. If you have any questions or concerns, let him know. Should hold muster on the pier shortly. I'll see you around. Good luck."

"Thanks, Chief. I got it," Corbett replied.

Chief Burgess had turned to leave as he quickly turned back. "Oh yeah. Try to stay clear of the XO for a while. I'll let him know that I have already talked to you. I assume you know why I'm suggesting that."

"Yeah COB. I understand. Thanks," Corbett replied as he returned to his seat on the piling of the pier and emptied his cup of cold coffee over the side. He reached for his shirt pocket to retrieve a cigarette. "Damn! I quit smoking months ago. Still have the habit," he mumbled to himself.

A noticeable addition to the sailors on the pier were the civilians. Wives and girlfriends stood with their men attempting to make small talk; holding, clinging but mostly crying. Their anguish was evident, anticipating the long months ahead alone; months which most had lived before, but few accepted as the norm.

A tall dark brunette in her early twenties with a small child came down the pier and embraced a sailor who had just crossed the gangway from the submarine. Corbett glanced in her direction and quickly made a double take. He rose quickly and turned his back to avoid recognition by the girl from Sloppy Joe's. He quickly hid himself in the crowd to avoid an embarrassing situation. He soon realized that her name was Julie, and she was the wife of his newly acquired friend, Don White. He momentarily felt an intense hatred for her. It quickly changed to sorrow for White, pity for her and hatred of himself. He was surprised when he realized what he was thinking. It wouldn't have made any difference if he had known who she was. He quickly discarded the thought and walked across the gangway back to his boat.

Executive Officer (XO), Lieutenant Commander Leonard Little, walked hurriedly down the pier and went aboard the boat. He was a tall man with a dark tan. He was called "Mary Poppins" by the crew because he always looked so neat and insisted the boat always be kept clean. He scheduled periods of clean-up every day and was quick to put any man on report he found sleeping when he should be cleaning. The scuttlebutt is that he wears his rank on the collar of his pajamas and requires his wife to salute him after each regularly scheduled evolution of sexual intercourse. He also has the reputation of being a hard-working, dedicated naval officer. Largely through his excellent efforts as XO, *(Redacted)* was awarded the battle efficiency "E" for excellence for the past two years. He has the misfortune of becoming the antagonist in the play of day to day life aboard ship. He is the relief valve which relieves the tensions accumulated in the crew which is a very necessary requirement.

He was soon to be followed aboard by the remaining nine junior officers of the wardroom. They quickly set about their tasks of checking their departments and divisions for readiness to go to sea.

"Now quarters for muster topside on the pier," blared over the announcing system. The men formed in ranks on the pier after reluctantly saying their last goodbyes. Information of a general nature was published at quarters, but not heard by many.

"Secure from quarters and station the maneuvering watch," the executive officer ordered.

The sailors hurried off in all directions to man their various stations. The submarine was readied for sea and awaited the arrival of the commanding officer. The Commanding Officer, Commander John L. Flynn, appeared from a parked car at the head of the pier with a female driver. He waved back without turning as he walked very slowly down the pier toward *(Redacted)*. He stopped once to pick up a penny lying on the ground and again to watch a school of fish swimming among the pilings along the pier. He threw the penny into the middle of the swimming fish.

Commander Flynn is a short, stocky middle-aged man. He has dark hair graying around the temples. He is a stern but fair man.

He expects and receives the best effort from the men under him. He wears the gold Dolphins signifying his qualification aboard submarines as well as the hard-earned insignia of a Navy Seal. His award ribbons on his khaki shirt include the Congressional Medal of Honor. The details of his heroic exploits are well known by only a few. He finally reached the gangway and crossed to the boat.

"Attention on deck!" the watch shouted.

"Carry on," the captain replied while returning the salute of all hands on deck.

"Ready for sea, Capt'n," the executive officer reported.

"Very well," he returned. "Let's get going."

The captain proceeded directly to the bridge area in the sail where he placed his set of binoculars around his neck. All the mooring lines were taken in and stowed, except the one at the bow. A young sailor hurried back across the gangway and gave his pregnant wife of eight months a final goodbye kiss and returned to the sub just as quickly.

The young officer of the deck (OOD) greeted the captain, "Good morning, Capt'n."

"Take us to sea, Barney," the captain replied. "Take note of the incoming morning tide at the harbor entrance. I don't want to have a tug pull us off the beach. That would ruin my day."

Aye, aye, Captain.

"Take in the gangway," the officer of the deck shouted from the bridge. "Take in number one line. Back one third."

The submarine backed slowly from the inboard submarine, turned in the middle of the channel and headed through the harbor entrance towards the open sea, picking up speed quickly. Families and friends stood waving on the pier. They were gone. The date was 5 May 1967.

The water in the channel was calm and reflected the bright rays of the sun. Steam, formed by the warm air in contrast with the cool water, rose very slowly and disappeared a few feet above the surface. The sleek black hull of the submarine cut a path through the maze of patchy fog on its way to its natural habitat, the open sea. The bow of the boat submerged and surfaced in a slow, rhythmic motion in step with a playful porpoise swimming alongside. The churning propeller created a trail of white, salty foam astern. *(Redacted)* would not have to travel far. Unlike many ports along the Atlantic coast, the continental shelf around Key West descended quickly into the ocean depths which allowed the boat to submerge safely. This feature made Key West a preferred port since it reduced transit time and provided more time for training exercises with aircraft, destroyers and other submarines.

Corbett was at his watch station as throttleman in the engine room. He stood next to the propulsion control panel in the maneuvering room and observed the operator. Soon, Corbett himself was shifting power supplies and controlling the boat's turbines like the professional he was.

The maneuvering room is the location where the nuclear reactor, electrical plant, and steam plant are controlled. It's a small area near the front of the engine room, manned by the engineering officer of the watch (EOW) and four enlisted crew members including an engineering leading petty officer (LPO). An enlisted man sits in front of each panel. The leading petty officer supervises the operation of the entire engine room.

The middle panel is manned by the reactor operator who controls the reactor temperature by adjusting the height of the nuclear reactor control rods. Subcooled hot water at an average temperature (TAV) of about 480 degrees and 2000 psi from the nuclear reactor circulates through the steam generators. (***Actual parameters are classified***). As steam is pulled from the steam generators to the turbines to increase the speed of the boat, it reduces the temperature of the water in the nuclear reactor. The nuclear reactor reacts automatically to the decrease in temperature and increasing the power level and temperature. The reactor operator raises the reactor control rods to assist, if necessary, the reactor and maintain a relatively constant TAV. He also controls the reactor coolant pumps. Cooling water flow must always be maintained through the reactor to prevent damage to the reactor core. With a total loss of cooling water, the reactor could experience a total reactor core melt down. In the unlikely event of a rupture of the reactor cooling water system, the reactor operator can close the coolant isolation valves to prevent a total loss of coolant. Recovery from this type of accident is extremely complicate and hopefully rare. The engine room personnel are constantly trained to react to this event.

The panel to the right in maneuvering is the electrical distribution panel manned by an electrical operator who controls the auxiliary turbine generators. The generators supply electricity to the distribution panels throughout the boat and the motor generators that either charge or use the battery during emergency propulsion. Power for the entire boat is provided from either the auxiliary turbines, emergency storage battery or shore power when along the pier in port.

The panel on the left is manned usually by another electrician or machinist mate who is qualified as throttleman and is in charge of the steam plant and speed of the boat. The throttleman's most important duty is to answer propulsion orders from control. When the officer of the deck (OOD) in control orders a new speed, the helmsman in control transfers the new order on the engine order telegraph next to him, which relays it back to the throttleman. The throttleman then spins the circular throttle at his panel which opens or closes the valves at the main engine turbines, allowing more or less steam to flow into them. The main steam turbine connects to the direct drive and single propeller.

The engineer, Lieutenant Eddy, is the EOW with Ensign Caldwell a junior officer in training under his supervision. Chief Sullivan supervises the remaining crew members in engineering.

"I'm glad to see you're learning fast," Sullivan remarked to Corbett.

"It's not that difficult," Corbett replied.

"We'll see how you can do before we let you go on your own. I'm sure you'll carry your part of the load before long. I want you to stand a few reactor control panel watches also as soon as possible. We can use some extra hands. I am sure you already know the electrical control panel like the back of your hand."

Obviously his LPO had not yet read his service record. Corbett is a qualified EOW and trained to operate all stations in the engine room including responding to all emergencies.

"I'm ready at any time Chief, just let me know," Corbett replied. Corbett watched as the short, heavy, chief petty officer turned and walked away. In the short period of time in which Corbett had known him, he had learned to like him very much.

Chief Petty Officer Sullivan is a good submariner. After twenty-nine years in the Navy, he was due to retire after the

(*Redacted*) completed its recent SUBSAFE overhaul. He was extended for this trip due to the shortage of personnel and the importance of the mission. He had served on the USS *Perch* (SS 209) during World War II and made four war patrols. Before the *Perch* departed on her fifth patrol, Sullivan was transferred. *Perch* never returned. She became one of the 52 submarines lost during World War II. During the late fifties, he served on Regulus missile submarines. In those four years, he was home with his family a total of ten months. Everyone wondered how he had time to father nine children during his naval career; all of which looked exactly like him.

"Corbett mind your station. Answer that speed order," Ensign Caldwell ordered.

"Aye, aye, Sir," Corbett replied as he smirked and pretended to open the turbine throttles. He had already complied with the speed order.

Third Class Petty Officer Jimmy Gene Johnson was standing watch on the electric distribution panel near Corbet. Petty Officer Johnson is an interior communications systems (IC) technician responsible under the supervision of Chief Sullivan for all instrument monitoring systems on the boat. It is a rating that requires an understanding of not only electronics but also a detailed knowledge of the systems that are monitored such as the reactor control instrumentation. Johnson is from Atlanta, Georgia and happens to be the only Black sailor onboard (*Redacted*). He is rather small in stature, weighs no more than 120 pounds soaking wet and five feet four inches tall. Because of his almost constant smile and happy go lucky attitude he is very well liked by all the crew but is often the target of kidding and practical jokes. He is called Jiminy Cricket, Jiminy or even Cricket for short, since he is often the sense of reason and contriteness among the crew. He does not hesitate to counsel members of the crew regarding their perceived bad conduct. His dungaree uniform trousers and shirt are neatly pressed. His shoes are spit shined with a glow reflected from the maneuvering room overhead light. He wears his white hat pushed to the back of his head and seldom takes it off except to sleep. He happens to have absolutely no teeth and wears a complete set of dentures which he often elects not to wear except to eat. They are understandably very uncomfortable.

Corbet leaned over in the direction of Johnson and whispered, "Is he that much of a pain-in-the-ass all of the time?"

Johnson smiled, leaned in and replied with his usual toothless grin, "He's new and just started his qualification as EOW. Have to cut him some slack until he's weaned from his mother tit."

Corbet grinned as he thought *"I really like this guy. He could be my new drinking buddy."*

A sailor with a somewhat angry look quickly entered maneuvering. "Cricket! Some of my plastic bags are missing. You been messing around in the ELT lab again.?"

"Don't get your skives tied in a knot, Kelly. I only took one," Johnson remarked as he reached up and took down a plastic bag lying on top of the electrical control panel. The plastic bag contained Johnson's dentures.

"I may not have enough bags to last the entire trip. I use those bags for contaminated samples. Now stay the fuck out of the lab or you will be one sorry son-of a-bitch."

"Now you know that you should not use such language, Kelly. Your mother would not…"

"Oh, just shut the fuck up, Cricket and stay out of the lab," Kelly interrupted as he stormed out of maneuvering.

Kelly is a machinist mate second class and is one of the engineering laboratory technicians responsible for the monitoring and detecting radioactive contamination aboard ship. Periodic swipes of all areas are analyzed using the equipment in the engineering laboratory located in the engine room. The most often used piece of equipment in the ELT lab is a short fat thick lead lined instrument referred as the Pig. A sample is placed in the Pig which electronically measures and identifies any dangerous alpha, beta or gamma radiation which may be present.

"Alright, now. Knock off the chatter and mind your watch stations people," Ensign Caldwell ordered.

"Aye, aye, Sir. No worries. Minding my station. Won't happen again, Sir," Johnson replied with a somewhat suppressed giggle which turned slowly into laughter. He was probably reacting to an image of the young ensign with a mother's tit in his mouth.

The EOW simply looked at Johnson with curiosity before turning to look in the other direction.

After securing from maneuvering watch, Sullivan went forward to the chief petty officer's quarters. A poker game had already started, and he didn't want to miss it.

"Guess what, Sully?" one of his fellow chief petty officers asked.

"What do you mean, guess what? What in the hell do you want?" Sullivan replied.

"You don't have to bite my head off. I just thought you might like to know that there are 40 cases of beer in the bow compartment."

"There's what, where?"

"Forty cases of that beautiful nectar."

"You're shitting me. Who told you that?" Sullivan continued.

"I saw it when they brought it aboard. It was the captain's idea."

"He must be getting soft," Sullivan remarked as he sat down at the table. "I've been on other boats that allowed booze on board for special occasions but not this one. No, never!"

"I'll show you," the chief added with a note of confidence. "Come on."

"Forget it. It'll only make me feel bad. I'll see it when I can pop the top. I'd like to see Mary Poppins' face when she finds out about it. It'll bust her girdle strings," Sullivan remarked with a laugh that shook his belly. "Shut up and deal."

On the bridge Commander Flynn rose from the seat which he was occupying, stretched, yawned loudly and spoke to the young officer of the deck (OOD). "Barney…when we reach point X-ray, you have permission to submerge the boat. We will proceed to a transit depth of 600 feet on a course of eight-zero degrees, speed 30 knots. Inform me when we reach the 100-fathom curve outbound. I'm going below. Don't hesitate to call me when in doubt."

"Aye, aye, Capt'n," the young officer replied.

Ensign Barney Pool is one of the nine junior officers aboard **(Redacted).** He recently married but their honeymoon had to be postponed due to the current unexpected deployment. He graduated from the Naval Academy prior to Officer Submarine School. He is assistant to the weapons officer responsible for the load of Mark 48 conventional and nuclear armed torpedoes. Like many of the other junior officers onboard, he quickly qualified as officer of the deck responsible on the bridge for the safety of the boat when steaming on the surface and as diving officer while submerged in the control room. In the control room, he supervises the diving planesman and helmsman to ensure that the boat maintains the correct course and depth submerged. He has not yet earned his gold Dolphins. His other duties include communications and commissary officer. He is due to be promoted to Lieutenant Junior Grade (LTJG) in a few months.

"Secure the maneuvering watch. Set the regular underway watch, section one," came over the announcing system as the captain entered the control room of the operations compartment.

He stopped at a control console and flipped on the microphone. "This is the Captain speaking. I can now provide you with additional information regarding our deployment. After the transfer of additional special operations personnel by helicopter near the Canary Islands, we will transit through the Straits of Gibraltar into the Mediterranean. We will conduct electronic recognizance along the North African coast. Intelligence has detected a large build-up of Egyptian, Syrian and Jordan military forces in the area. Our job is to determine to the extent possible the objectives of these recent military exercises and deployments. I anticipate that our deployment will be approximately three to four months."

Men throughout the submarine stopped in their tracks and listened.

"I might add that each man will receive a ration of beer each Saturday," the captain continued.

Cheers could be heard coming from the various compartments.

"I'll take your ration, Mary. Your wife won't let you drink," an unknown sailor shouted.

The executive officer muttered something and closed the door to his stateroom.

The captain secured the microphone and headed for his stateroom.

The submarine was suddenly filled with the sound of the collision alarm. The siren whined as all watertight doors separating the compartments slammed shut. All hands jumped to their feet, grabbed the damage control equipment and waited for the announcement of the location of the collision or flooding.

The captain flew from his stateroom to the control room and swung the periscope in all directions as the submarine slowly stopped dead in the water. "What the hell?" the captain remarked as he lowered the periscope and climbed the ladder to the bridge.

"I'm sorry, Capt'n," the young officer of the deck remarked. "I rang the collision alarm by mistake. I meant to sound the diving alarm to submerge."

The captain shook his head in disbelief. "That's once, Mister Pool. You don't get three strikes in my ball game," the captain said very sternly.

"Aye, aye, Sir," the young officer replied.

"Secure from collision, Barney. Come to my stateroom after you get off watch. I want a full report on the actions of the crew. It was a good drill anyway," the captain said with an unexpected smile. "I'm going below. Don't hesitate to call me when in doubt."

"Aye, aye, Capt'n," the officer returned, smiling.

The captain slapped the young officer on the behind and slipped down the hatch. The word was passed, and *(Redacted)* slowly picked up speed as all compartments secured from the evolution.

"Dive! Dive!" blared over the announcing system as the klaxon sounded. The klaxon is a relic from the WWII submarines but carried on some modern submarines as a tribute to their legacy.

The boat slipped beneath the surface of the ocean as the chief of the watch in control opened the main vents and air in the main ballast tanks was replaced by sea water. The officer of the deck manned the periscope in control while Ensign Pool manned his station as the diving officer. The lookouts down from the bridge took their positions at the diving and steering controls.

"At six-zero feet, Sir," the depth control planesman reported, pulling back slightly on his depth control stick.

"Very well," the diving officer acknowledged.

"At six-zero feet, Sir. Trim is satisfactory," the diving officer reported to the officer of the deck swinging quickly on the periscope.

"Very well. Make your depth six-zero-zero feet smartly. Make turns for 30 knots. Steer course zero-eight-zero degrees."

Each man in the control room carried out their orders working as a team which came only after hours of training.

Throughout the boat, the men settled down to establish the routine which they would follow for many days. Some played cards, some read, most slept; but all were quiet. The first day underway was always spent remembering faces which could only be seen in photographs for many weeks. It was not a good life; it was not a bad life; it was a submarine sailor's life.

SitRep 2-Spec Ops Mission

The submarine cruised mile after mile, day after day far beneath the surface of the ocean; free from the stormy elements which have plagued mariners since man first ventured into the ocean's environment. In the auxiliary machinery space, the oxygen (O_2) generator separated the compound water (H_2O) into the elements of oxygen and hydrogen. Carbon dioxide (CO_2) scrubbers discharged the harmful gas overboard replaced by the life-giving oxygen for breathing. In the nuclear reactor compartment, the heart of the submarine was steadily beating. In a submicroscopic world, nuclear uranium material in the reactor disintegrated in millions of tiny explosions converting mass to energy in the form of heat. From the heat came steam from the steam generators to turn the steam turbines supplying the vital electricity; nuclear, thermal, mechanical and electrical energy combined in the true submersible; limited only by man's endurance.

Deployment 6 Days

The date is 11 May 1967. "Control…this is radio. We are in communications with the helicopter Whiskey Two. They are inbound from the Canary Islands. ETA in thirty minutes."

"Radio… this is control. Send our position to Whiskey Two."

"Captain…control. We have the helicopter inbound. Permission to surface for personnel transfer?"

"Control…this is the Captain. Negative…remain submerged. Direct Seal Team Charlie to transfer aboard in accordance with Plan Bravo. Station the recovery team at the forward access hatch."

"Aye, aye, Captain."

The Seal Team consisted of six men. They dropped from the helicopter 5,000 yards from *(Redacted)*. They covered that distance submerged quickly and entered the bow compartment through the forward access hatch. The captain and executive officer greeted the team as they came down the ladder from the access hatch.

"Welcome aboard," the captain remarked. "Who is the team leader?"

"Lieutenant Kingsley reporting aboard with your permission, Captain," the first member of the team replied.

"This is my XO and he will show you to your assigned bunks," the captain explained. "I'm sure that you are anxious to get out of those wet suits and into some dry warm clothes. We'll go over the details of your mission after you get settled. We should have all of your equipment on board."

"I assume that we are invited to stay for dinner," the lieutenant remarked with a smile.

"Certainly," the captain replied. "Best food prepared by the best cook in the fleet. Sorry Lieutenant ...we had to revert to Plan Bravo for your transfer," the captain explained. "We have reports of reconnaissance aircraft in the area and could not risk detection on the surface."

"No problem, Captain. That's what we do for exercise," the lieutenant replied with a smile as he turned and accompanied the XO to the berthing compartment.

After quickly taking onboard the seal team near the Canary Islands, *(Redacted)* continued on course and entered the Mediterranean through the Straits of Gibraltar.

54

Deployment-10 Days

On 15 May 1967 *(Redacted)* reached her destination. "Now man battle stations," came over the announcing system, followed by the gong of the general alarm. The boat suddenly came alive as men rushed to their stations.

"Rig control for red," the captain ordered.

"Aye, aye, Sir," the order was acknowledged.

"I have the conn, make your depth six-zero feet smartly, ahead standard," the captain continued as he raised the periscope.

The boat rose quickly but remained hidden just below the surface. The captain swung the periscope around very quickly and observed the horizon as the mast broke the surface. It was dark but sunrise was quickly approaching. As the periscope rotated, land was visible in the distance and appeared as a silhouette against the moon lite sky. A small mountain range descended sharply to sea level below.

"I have the transmission tower on the ridge blinking thirty seconds on and one minute off. Mark the range, mark the bearing, down periscope," ordered the captain in rapid succession.

"Range twenty-six miles, bearing zero-seven-zero degrees, Captain."

"My compliments to the navigator. We are only two miles off our rendezvous point. No shipping contacts in the area. Have all hands secure from battles stations except for the tracking party. Leonard, you and I will take turns on watch in control for the first couple of days. You'll have the first watch. Commence the patrol routine."

"Aye, aye, Captain," the executive officer replied. "Raise the ECM and radar masts. Up periscope."

The captain proceeded to the control console and flipped on the general announcing system microphone. "This is the captain speaking. We are currently off the Egyptian coast city of Alexandria. Our patrol area will be from Alexandria in the west to Port Said and Haifa along the Gaza Strip to the east. We will observe all military operations in the area as well as merchant shipping entering the major ports. We are directed to classify all electronic communications and countermeasure signals along the coast. We will be on station for approximately three months. We are joined by one other conventional submarine in the area as well as an AGTR surface vessel. I am confident that every man will do his job and our mission will be a total success. That is all." The captain proceeded forward to his quarters.

Patrol Area of USS *(Redacted)*

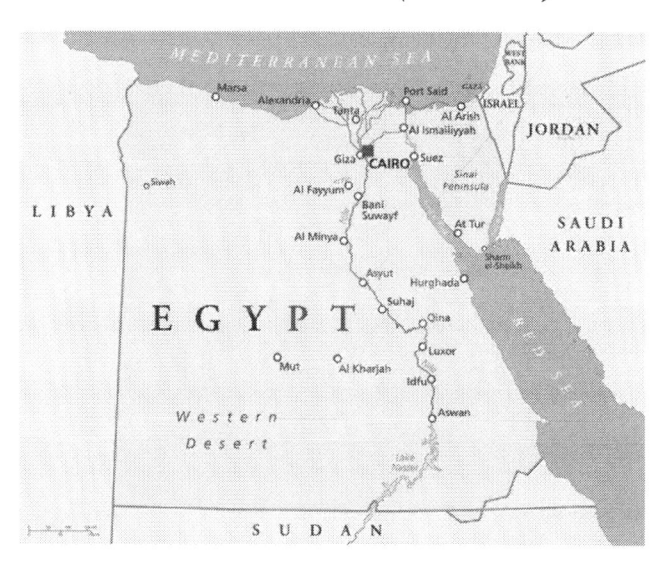

The radar and electronic counter measure masts were raised and broke the water just above the surface. An electronics technician and two special operations personnel in the ECM room and radar manned the intelligence equipment and analyzed the many signals appearing on the equipment scopes. The executive officer seemed nervous as he observed the surface through the periscope.

"The periscope is underwater. Get back on ordered depth," he ordered.

The depth control planesman pulled the control stick back and slowly brought the boat to a shallow depth. Seaman Wallace stood behind the planesman watching the operation of the planes. After a few moments, he slid into pilot chair to operate the planes for his final qualification. The chief of the watch in control would observe and evaluate his performance.

"Sonar contact, bearing three-one-five degrees," suddenly came over the intercom unit from the sonar room.

At the same time, in control a junior machinist mate fireman in the A-Gang was on watch at the trim and drain station for training. He received a request from the engine room to pump bilges and started the bilge pump without prior permission from the chief of the watch in control.

Sonar picked up the unexpected noise and reported, "Control…possible torpedo in the water astern, Sir."

The executive officer quickly lowered the periscope. "Emergency deep! Take her down! Ahead full! Full dive on the diving planes!" he ordered.

The submarine took a steep down angle and quickly picked up speed. The down angle became greater as the depth increased.

57

The men throughout the boat held on to anything available to prevent being hurled forward.

"Level off," the executive officer ordered to the diving officer. "You're getting too large an angle."

"Planes jammed in full dive!" Wallace shouted from his seat at the diving controls. He worked quickly to shift the diving planes to manual and restore the operation to normal. He pulled the control stick to the full raise position in an attempt to correct the large down angle, but it was too late.

The depth indicator on the diving station was spinning fast. The down angle of the submarine quickly reached sixty degrees as it passed a depth of 1,000 feet. Toolboxes, bookcases and benches slid to the forward end of the compartments. Coffee cups shattered on the decks. Pots of food cooking in the galley splashed against the bulkhead. As the down angle became even greater, larger pieces of equipment began to move. The holding straps on a torpedo in the bow compartment parted. The torpedo slid harmlessly to the forward bulkhead just missing a sailor as he jumped clear. An unsecured, sharp piece of deck plating came loose in the auxiliary machinery space, flew into the next compartment and lodged in an instrument panel. Men lying in their bunks were in the safest locations and were almost vertical.

"Oh shit! We've had it," came from a voice somewhere in the control room.

"Blow the forward ballast tanks, left full rudder, back full," the executive officer shouted as he held fast to a railing at the periscope stand.

The helmsman at the diving station was not strapped in and was thrown low into his seat with the excessive down angle. He struggled but could not reach the ship's speed enunciator to order back full on the propulsion turbines.

In maneuvering, Corbett was on watch at the propulsion control panel. He had already realized the excessive down angle was abnormal and quickly placed the steam turbines to the astern position. The boat shook violently as the propeller cut into the water, slowly pulling the boat to a stop and leveling off. The outer hull of the submarine creaked and made a groaning noise under the extreme sea pressure. Corbett noticed the pressure gage on the bulkhead that indicated a depth of nearly 1,500 feet. The boat was near what was expected to be crush depth. As soon as the boat gained an up angle after its decent, Corbett reversed the turbine throttles and made turns for ahead full speed. The submarine proceeded quickly toward the surface.

Chief Sullivan was EOW on watch in the maneuvering room and had been thrown from his seat out of maneuvering across the engine room during the excessive down angle. He was able to regain his seat at his watch station and reported, "Control…maneuvering making turns for 20 knots."

The diving officer in control responded, "Very well maneuvering."

Chief Sullivan turned to Corbett, patted him on the back and said with a big thank you smile, "Thanks shipmate. You probably saved our bacon."

Corbett lowered his head and replied, "Well Chief, you may have to save mine now. It remains to be seen if I did the right thing. I'm sure you know hindsight is 20/20. I could be in deep shit."

In control, the executive officer had also been thrown from his watch station at the periscope stand but managed to return after the boat had achieved an up angle heading toward the surface.

The captain finally succeeded in his attempt to make it into the control room. "What in the hell happened?" he shouted.

"Planes jammed in the full dive position, Sir," the executive officer reported. "I have it under control and proceeding back to a shallow depth. We exceeded test depth."

"Flooding in the engine room… flooding in the engine room!" blared over the intercom.

All watertight doors slammed shut as the siren sounded. Sound powered phones were manned in all compartments.

The chief of the watch at the ballast panel in control reported, "Engine room reports the flooding has been secured. A small sea water line ruptured."

"Very well," the captain acknowledged. "What is your depth now?"

"Depth one-zero-zero-zero feet, Sir and coming up."

"Control…this is the operations officer in sonar. The identified torpedo was apparently the bilge pump that started."

The captain turned to the executive officer and said, "Get back to periscope depth, get yourself relieved and report to my stateroom. Find out from maneuvering who has the watch at the propulsion panel and send him to my stateroom. Also have the operations and engineering officer report to me now," the captain ordered. What I just witnessed was totally FUBAR (*Fucked Up by All Recognition*) and far beyond any reasonable explanation." He turned and stormed out of the control room.

The boat returned to periscope depth. Men in the various compartments went to work stowing equipment. The loose torpedo was secured in its rack. The weapons officer would surely be reprimanded or even relieved if the forth coming investigation shows that the nuclear armed weapon was not secured properly.

The executive officer reluctantly reported to the captain's stateroom.

"What was the cause of the loss of depth control?" the captain asked.

The XO stood rigid as he spoke, "We picked up a sonar contact and sonar incorrectly reported a torpedo in the water. I ordered emergency deep. There was an inexperienced man at the planes. He jammed the depth control planes in the full dive position."

"What type of sonar contact did you have?"

The officer hesitated. "I don't know, Sir. I thought it was a patrol boat. There are no ships visible on the surface now. I guess it's gone, Sir."

"Do you mean you ordered emergency deep on an unclassified contact? It could have been a whale for all you know. With no additional fire control reports, you should have known that the sonar report of a sudden torpedo launch was a mistake."

"Yes, Sir. That's true. I realize I made a mistake. If there had been a more experienced planesman and diving officer..."

"Don't try to shift the blame," the captain interrupted. "You were in charge. You are responsible."

"Yes, Sir."

"Return to your station and thank God that you didn't kill us all."

The captain had adhered to the cardinal rule praise your officers in public and criticize in private.

The XO turned and walked out of the stateroom without a word. He realized that he had made a mistake. He was unreliable in the eyes of the captain. He must try hard to erase the black mark on his image.

Corbett knocked on the captain's door and entered. "Petty Officer Corbet, Sir. You wanted to see me, Captain?"

"Yes, Corbett, come in. I understand you had the watch on the propulsion control panel and backed the boat on your own initiative."

"Yes, Sir, I did. Sorry, Capt'n. It was an impulse reaction that just kicked in and I didn't even really have a chance to think about it."

"I want you to know I am certain that if it weren't for your actions; we might have exceeded collapse depth."

"I'm glad that you think it was necessary, Capt'n. I'm sure anyone would have done the same thing."

"They might have but you did. I'm recommending you for a commendation. It appears that you were the only person on board that actually did his job. Well done. You recently reported aboard if I remember correctly. The COB said that you were an instructor at the S1W at Arco."

"Yes, that's true, Capt'n."

"I thought you look familiar. You were training prospective commanding officers in EOW classes. I was in one of your accelerated classes."

"Yes, Sir. I do remember you."

"The commanding officer of the *Thresher* was also in our class. Remarkable officer. He will always be remembered."

"And all members of the crew," Corbett replied as lowered his head in respect. "I knew many of the crew personally. A best friend of mine was onboard."

The captain showed some emotion when he smiled and stated, "That's all, Corbett. If we have the chance, we must talk again. You're dismissed."

"Thank you, Sir." Corbett replied with a smile. As he left the stateroom, he mumbled to himself, "That was a surprise."

As Corbett left, the operations and engineering officer had been waiting and entered the captain's stateroom. The captain's angry voice can barely be heard coming from his stateroom. It was obvious that the two officers were not being commended for the mistakes that were made by the people they supervised.

The captain picked up the sound powered phone in his stateroom and called, "Navigator this is the Captain. We are required to file an incident report with ComSubLant regarding the depth excursion. Draft up the message for my signature stating that we exceeded test depth due a loss of depth control planes during routine drills. Fill any other details which you deem appropriate in accordance with the incident report procedures."

"Aye, aye, Captain," the navigator replied.

In the control room the chief of the watch mentioned to Wallace, "You did good, Sailor. Your recovery from the jammed planes was excellent and prevented an even larger down angle. I don't think the jam was your fault. Thermal down currents on the planes can cause that also. I will give you a well done to the COB on your qualification report."

"Thanks, Chief. I appreciate that," Wallace replied with a sigh of relief.

Later that morning, the captain entered the wardroom and sat at the table. The steward was quick to follow with his usual cup of coffee. Several junior officers were also sitting around the table. They all appeared to be concentrating on the books which they were reading and avoided his glances. The captain flipped the switch on the intercom unit next to him and spoke to the executive officer in control.

"XO, this is the Captain. Since this is Saturday, I think you should get a bingo game started for the crew after lunch and pass out the ration of beer."

"Captain, this is our first day on station and I don't think a bingo game would be wise," the executive officer replied.

"The men have worked hard this past week and they're expecting their beer ration," the captain returned.

After a pause, the executive officer said, "I did have a field day scheduled this afternoon."

The captain glanced around the wardroom. The officers were staring at him and listening attentively. They quickly looked away when discovered.

"Your recommendation has been received and considered, set up the bingo game and pass out the beer ration after the noon meal," he said and turned off the intercom unit without an acknowledgement.

After a few seconds word was passed over the announcing system, "Now there will be a bingo game after the noon meal. Each man, not on watch, will draw his beer ration in the bow compartment."

Cheers erupted from the men in the various compartments.

"Now field day will be delayed until 1430," soon followed over the announcing system.

A round of boos accompanied the announcement. The captain rose from his chair and walked to his stateroom. Low muffled curse words could be heard in the passageway as the captain spoke over the sound powered phone. He returned shortly and sat down.

"Now field day is canceled today," was passed and was once again followed by a round of cheers and whistles.

After the noon meal the sound powered phones were manned in each compartment. The COB passed out bingo cards for 50 cents each. The proceeds would go to the boat's recreation fund. A man in the control room drew the numbers and relayed them to the other compartments.

Corbett and Chief Sullivan sat at a table in the crew's mess, sipped their beer and placed the numbers on their cards.

"I think you got the shaft when they made you go on this trip, Chief," Corbett said. "How can you take it and not be bitter?"

"It all counts on 30 years, kid. Don't worry about it," Sullivan replied as he lifted his bottle of beer and announced a toast. "Here's to that great American statesman and son-of-a-bitch, Josephus Daniels."

"To Josephus," everyone shouted in unison.

Corbett quickly raised his bottle and took a long drink. "Who in hell is Josephus Daniels?" he asked while wiping spilled beer from his chin and on the table.

Sullivan raised his bottle and watched the bubbles forming in his beer. "Josephus Daniels, Secretary of the Navy, from 1913 until 1921. He decided that sailors shouldn't drink while at sea, that dirty son of a bitch. No women and no booze, it's a hell of a life."

"I guess you're glad to be retiring soon?" Corbett asked.

"Yes, I am," Sullivan replied. "But not for the reasons you think."

"What do you mean, Chief?"

"It's hard to explain," Sullivan replied. "I guess it's the atmosphere of the Navy today. I'm set in my ways and I can't adjust to change."

"In what way?"

"I guess you hear every day about the good old days," Sullivan continued. "I truly like and miss the old Navy and I can't help but dislike what's happening. Petty officers have no authority or respect anymore. The kids coming in the Navy are mostly losers because they receive very little discipline at home. You try to kick their ass and square them away and they go screaming to mama. The next thing you know you have congressman and the old man on your back."

"I don't think it's that bad," Corbett replied.

"Guess you'll learn the hard way," Sullivan said. "The worst thing is the differences and bad feelings between the nuclear and non-nuke sailors onboard. The non-nukes feel like the engineering nukes are stuck on themselves and are not actually submarine sailors. I understand. I felt the same before I decided to go to Nuclear Power School and became leading PO. The nuke boats are a very necessary and inevitable change, but you can't duplicate the comradery aboard the old smoke boats. I miss that most of all."

"I try to treat everyone the same," Corbett replied. "Give respect where respect is due, I always say. Kinda corny but they are all my brothers if they wear the Dolphins or working their ass off to earn them. The strict regulations aboard nuclear submarines are probably necessary because of the reactor driven tea kettle back aft."

"I agree with you on the regulation part," Chief Sullivan replied. "But you have to admit the regs are getting out of hand to some extent. The guys can't even vent and say fuck it without fear of being placed on report which I have reluctantly had to do on more than one occasion."

"Like you said, old man. All counts on 30. Hey, I won!" Corbett shouted. "I mean, Bingo! I just won two more beers. How about that?"

Sullivan picked up Corbett's card and rose from the table. "Thanks, kid. You're too young to drink that much."

"Hey," Corbett said. "That's my card, Sully."

"Remember what I said about respecting your seniors. You can call me chief, sonny. Let this be a lesson. Never get excited about anything and you'll never be disappointed," Sullivan remarked with a grin and hurried to the bow compartment to claim his ill-gotten prize.

As Sullivan departed, White entered the compartment, seeing Corbett; he waved, walked to his seat and sat down. "How's it going, ole buddy?" he asked.

"Can't complain. How's it been with you?" Corbett returned.

"The same, I guess. How's come we haven't talked much lately? If I didn't know any better, I'd say you were trying to avoid me."

"That's crazy, "Corbett said avoiding his glance. "I've been busy that's all."

One of the special operations personnel entered the crew's mess and sat next to White. He was dressed in Army fatigues but with no branch of service or rank insignia. "How's it going? Win anything yet?" he asked.

"Guess you could say that," Corbett answered with a grin. "So, what's with you? See you are not playing or drinking. Don't like beer?"

"Not that I don't like it. Not allowed to drink," he replied.

"Damn! That's too bad," White replied with a smile. "You win and I'll drink it for you."

"My name is Corbett. Glad to have you aboard. You Army…Marines…or what?" he asked. "You have no name tag, rank or rate on your uniform."

"My name is Pete. Can't tell you my branch of service or rank. If I did, I'd have to kill you," he said with a laugh.

"You spooks, much too secretive," White remarked.

"I've got to get going you guys," Corbett interrupted as he finished the last of his beer. "Nice meeting you Pete if that is your real name. Talk to you later, White."

"Hey, I've got a great idea. When we get back, how's about coming over to my place for dinner? My wife is a great cook and a barrel of laughs. I bet you two would hit it off great."

"Sure," Corbett replied. "Anytime you say."

"Any night except the first night back in port," White remarked with a laugh. "That's sort of special, if you know what I mean."

"Yeah, I understand," Corbett returned as he stood and walked away. "I guess I'd better get some shut eye before my afternoon watch. I'll see you later."

"Sure, buddy. See you later."

Corbett had been avoiding him. He regretted that White could no longer be his friend, but his shipmate's personal problems were his own and he could not get involved. The idea of meeting his wife socially at some point did not appeal to him either.

The days were uneventful as *(Redacted)* proceeded with its mission. The spec ops group spent long hours identifying the radar and countermeasure signals along the coast.

Deployment-31 Days

The date is 5 June 1967. The boredom of the crew was interrupted.

The captain entered the control room and flipped on the microphone of the general announcing system. "This is the Captain. We just received word that Israel has conducted a preemptive attack on the forces of Egypt, Jordan, Syria and Iraq. Most of the Egyptian air force has been destroyed. We have expected this conflict was coming for many months. You can guess now the reason behind our current mission. As of now, we have been given no orders concerning our rules of engagement in this conflict. The United States is officially neutral and a non-participant. I anticipate that we will be ordered to pull back from the immediate area at some point. Until that time, we will continue with our assignment. Be aware that we are in a war zone. If we or any other submarine is detected, we are a legitimate target. We will be at battle stations for some time. That is all."

"Now man battle stations…now man battle stations," blared over the general announcing system. Sound powered phones were quickly manned in each compartment. Men rushed fore and aft in the passageways to reach their assigned stations. Training would be at a minimum since the most experienced personnel would be required at the critical operating stations.

The seal team leader Lieutenant Kingsley knocked on the door of captain's stateroom and entered. "Captain, my team will disembark within the next four hours. With the latest developments our mission has been modified and we will be hitting the beach sooner than expected. Thanks very much for all of your assistance."

"Pleasure having you and your team aboard," the captain returned. "I am sure that you cannot discuss your new assignment in any more detail, so I won't ask. I'll just say good luck. I'll tell the COB to get some men together to help with your gear. I'll talk to the navigator and see if we can get you within 10,000 yards of the beach but can't promise to get you any closer than that."

Just as they came aboard while *(Redacted)* remained submerged, the seal team disembarked by the forward hatch for their swim ashore. Everyone was told that the United States would remain neutral and not participate in the current conflict. The extent of the country's involvement would become clearer in the coming days.

The following day, a radioman delivered a message to the captain's stateroom. "Message decoded Top Secret-For Your Eyes Only," he said.

He read the message carefully and then read it over again to make sure he understood correctly. "Very well," he said to the messenger. "Have the communications officer acknowledge receipt."

"Aye, aye, Capt'n," the messenger replied as he turned sharply and left the stateroom.

Later the captain called a conference of all his department heads in the wardroom.

"Gentlemen we have been directed by ComSixthFleet to deploy Ivanhoe against specified cargo ships enroute to Port Said and the Suez Canal. Intelligence has determined that advanced surface to air missiles are being delivered to the Egyptians. Our mission is to disable these cargo ships far out at sea before they reach port. I want your best men at their stations during sonar tracking stations. We haven't conducted this exercise in a while, but I am sure the crew will get it done."

"What national flag will the cargo ships be flying?" one of the junior officers asked.

"I was told, and you shouldn't ask," the captain replied. "That is strictly on a need to know basis and has no bearing on our mission. I am sure some will guess, and you are free to do so. Brief your LPOs as necessary gentlemen. As always, I am sure the crew will do fine. You are dismissed."

"Station the sonar tracking party…now station the sonar tracking party," came over the general announcing system from control.

The captain was shortly on station at the periscope in the control room. "I have the Conn. Diving Officer, make you depth six zero feet smartly," he ordered.

"Six-zero feet, Aye, Sir," the diving officer replied.

The planesman repeated the order as he pulled back the depth control stick." The boat sailed quickly upward from 600 feet. At six-zero feet, Sir," the planesman reported as he reached the ordered depth.

The captain turned the periscope around slowly several times as he spoke to the young man at the diving planes. "Wallace, I understand that you just recently completed your qualifications. Congratulations. I see that you are already wearing your new Dolphins on your dungaree shirt. I guess you want to show them off early."

"Yes. Guess you could say that, Capt'n," Wallace answered. "Can't wait till I'm wearing my dress uniform. That could be awhile."

"You don't have much experience on the planes yet, but I understand that you come highly recommended as the best man for this job by your leading petty officer. Is that right, Sailor?" the captain asked.

"Well, Sir, I only know that this is my sonar tracking and battle stations assignment. I appreciate the confidence the chief has in me, Sir and I will do my best."

"The Captain replied in a stern voice, "Sailor, I want a hell of a lot more than your best tonight. If I say depth six-zero and a half feet, that is what I expect. Not sixty or sixty-one. If we go emergency deep, I expect you to hit your mark. Is that understood?"

The young sailor hesitated, swallowed several times and replied, "Understood, Sir."

"Just stay focused son and you will do fine," the captain said with confidence. "Yes soiree. Fine as wine and twice as nice," the captain continued as a whisper only he could hear. It was one of the captain's favorite often used glib remarks.

The captain swung the periscope quickly around several times and ordered, "Sonar… give me a report on that surface contact." The captain waited for a response for a few moments that didn't come. "Don't make me ask again and have to say please sonar. I would not appreciate that!"

"Sorry, Captain…this is sonar, bearing one- five-zero degrees… speed 15 knots… course one-four-zero degrees … range 10,000 yards. Contact classified merchant. Keel depth on that merchant is three-zero feet Captain."

"ECM… I understand that you have identified that contact?" the captain continued.

"This is ECM…Roger Captain. We intercepted her movement report and cargo manifest. That is our target," returned over the speaker. "Her destination is the port of Sharm el-Sheikh."

"Roger? The captain thought with a grin. Must be a darn spec op spook Airdale. Thinks he's in an airplane."

"Very well ECM. Well done," the captain replied.

"Plot… this is the Captain. Give me a course and speed to intercept the target."

(Redacted) quickly intercepted the merchant ship and slowly positioned itself under the stern of the ship. A mast rose slowly from *(Redacted)*'s superstructure. A boron nitride covered titanium metal cylinder sat above the heavily reinforced mast like a jousting spear of a valiant knight. The knight was called Ivanhoe. Ivanhoe was raised slowly until it contacted the cargo ship's propeller. *(Redacted)* shook slightly and rolled from side to side from the shock as it made contact. The blades of the cargo ship's propeller were blasted apart like wood and the cargo ship came to an unexpected stop. Her cargo would not reach Sharm el-Sheikh.

(Redacted) quickly dove undetected to the safety of the ocean and proceeded to stalk its next target. Over the next several days, *(Redacted)* would intercept and disable two additional cargo ships. After each mission, an Israeli warship would soon arrive, board the disabled ship and confiscate its cargo before being towed to the nearest Israeli port. As many members of submarines on patrol often do, Quartermaster Rankin was secretly able to obtain copies of the patrol report photos of the confiscated cargo ships for his scrapbook as well as the attack on the ATGR which occurred the following day.

Deployment-34 Days

It was day 34 at sea for the crew of ***(Redacted)*** while for the rest of the world it was June 8, 1967.

"Reveille! Reveille! Up all hands. Clean sweep down fore and aft. Bag all trash for dumping," suddenly blared over the general announcing system, followed by "First call…first call to breakfast."

Corbett was just getting off his watch in the engine room and sat a table in the crew's mess. It was unusually quiet. Lee sat across from him. "How's it going with your qualifications, Lee?" Corbett asked.

"It an't going at all," Lee replied.

"Okay what is your problem? You behind on your quals?" Corbett returned.

"No problem," he replied. "I just can't hack it. I'm getting off this boat as soon as we get back. I have requested a mine sweeper out of Norfolk."

"Sorry to hear that. Wish I could change your mind. Think I could go to bat for you with your leading PO and the captain. Get you caught up on your system qualifications? What do you say?" Corbett asked.

"Fuck you and that white horse you rode in on!" Lee responded with a frown; as he got up, picked up his half-eaten food plate and left the table.

"We'll have to address your filthy mouth later… Sailor," Corbet replied to Lee as he walked away.

Snell moved over in front of Corbett at the table. "You're wasting your time with him," Snell remarked. "He's a lost cause."

Johnson was sitting and listening next to Snell and remarked, "No one is a lost cause."

"Darn, Cricket. That's what I was just thinking. Right you are!" Corbett replied.

"That boy has some serious issues but nothing a little mentoring wouldn't fix," Johnson continued. "He's definitely off on the wrong foot so to speak."

"Just heard some weird scuttlebutt from Rankin," Snell stated with excitement. "The ATGR on patrol with us was attacked by aircraft and patrol boats. Heard it was the USS *Liberty*. They think it might have been the Israelis."

"That's bull shit," Corbett replied. "That can't be true. We're on their side. Must be friendly fire."

"That's all I know. I understand we have periscope photographs of the attack," Snell replied.

"I'm sure we plan to help the *Liberty*," Corbet stated in a confused tone. "If not this a bunch of political bull shit. I am going to see what more I can find out," he said in a determined voice as he got up from the table and went forward.

The next day the following news report came in over the teletype and was released:

"On June 8, 1967 Israeli aircraft and torpedo boats attacked the USS Liberty in international waters off Egypt's Gaza Strip. The intelligence ship, well-marked as an American vessel and only lightly armed, was attacked first by Israeli aircraft that fired

napalm and rockets at the ship. The Liberty attempted to radio for assistance, but the Israeli aircraft blocked the transmissions. Eventually, the ship was able to make contact with the U.S. carrier Saratoga, and 12 fighter jets and four tanker planes were dispatched to defend the Liberty. When word of their deployment reached Washington, however, Secretary of Defense Robert McNamara ordered them recalled to the carrier, and they never reached the Liberty. The reason for the recall remains unclear."

"Back in the Mediterranean, the initial air raid against the Liberty was over. Nine of the 294 crew members were dead and 60 were wounded. Suddenly, the ship was attacked by Israeli torpedo boats, which launched torpedoes and fired artillery at the ship. Under the command of its wounded Captain, William L. McGonagle, the Liberty managed to avert four torpedoes, but one struck the ship at the waterline. Heavily damaged, the ship launched three lifeboats, but these were also attacked–a violation of international law. Failing to sink the Liberty, which displaced 10,000 tons, the Israelis finally desisted. In all, 34 Americans were killed and 171 were wounded in the two-hour attack. In the attack's aftermath, the Liberty is making its way to a safe port." Publisher A&E Television Networks

The crew of *(Redacted)* took the news some with angry, others with confusion and doubt. The general feeling was that the sailors aboard the ATGR had been abandoned by those who swore to defend them. The same could very well happen to them.

On June 11th, Israel announced a cease fire had been negotiated but *(Redacted)* continued its surveillance of the North African coast for another three months. Its mission was to determine if the Arab countries were regrouping their forces for a counterattack. A counterattack never occurred, and the cease fire held.

Deployment-138 Days

It is 20 September 1967. Word came over the general announcing system. "This is the Captain. We have received a message from ComSubLant via ComSixthFleet. We are released from our current assignment and congratulated on a job well done. Our deployment has, however, been extended. The *Skipjack* is experiencing equipment problems and is unable to perform its current mission. As always, *(Redacted)* has been assigned to take up the slack. From the Med, we will transient the Aegean and Marara Seas through the Bosporus Strait into the Black Sea. We will remain undetected and conduct reconnaissance in and around the Russian Naval Base at Sevastopol. The details of the recon will be passed to various divisions and petty officers on a need to know basis. We will now proceed to the port of Souda Bay, Crete to resupply and take onboard several additional special operations personnel. Sorry men. No liberty in Souda Bay. We will enter port under the cover of darkness and depart before sunrise. We will be on station until our mission is complete. After this mission we will not be returning to Key West. Our home port has been changed again back to Norfolk. The XO will make available all the info you will need to make arrangements for your families in Key West. Any questions will be addressed by your department heads. Sorry guys but shit happens. As always…just suck it up."

Sevastopol is on the shores of Black Sea and which is a sea between Southeast Europe and Western Asia. It is bounded by Europe, Anatolia and the Caucasus and drains through the Mediterranean into the Atlantic Ocean, via the Aegean Sea and various straits. The Bosporus Strait connects it to the Sea of Marmara, and the Strait of the Dardanelles connects that sea to the Aegean Sea region of the Mediterranean. These waters separate Eastern Europe and Western Asia. The Black Sea is also connected to the Sea of Azov by the Strait of Kerch. This will be the home of (***Redacted***) for several months.

Soviet Base at Sevastopol Ukraine

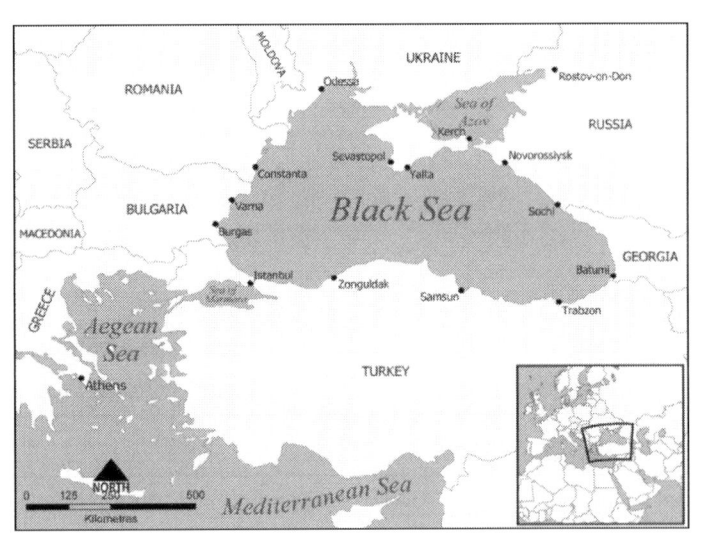

Rankin entered the crew's mess from the control room, drew a cup of coffee from a large pot and sat next to Wallace. "We been at sea for over four months now, so how's it hangin' there Wally?" he asked.

"How's it hanging? How is what hanging?" Wallace asked with a true since of confusion.

"Never mind, Wally," Corbett interrupted from across the table. "Just a rhetorical question. He doesn't know that you are still a virgin and wouldn't know about things like that."

"Who said I was a virgin?" Wallace asked. "That's nobody's business."

"Only a virgin spends less than a minute pounding his pud in his rack every night," Rankin replied with a long laugh.

Robishaw spoke up from an adjacent table. "Better not be doing that shit in your bunk, Wally," he said with a stern look. "My bunk is just below yours. Go to the head and join Beebe in a circle jerk if you get that horny."

"That's bullshit," Barnes replied as he looked up the from the sink where he was washing dishes.

Petty Officer Thomas stuck his head out of the galley and shouted, "You using hot water to wash those dishes? If not, I'm going to kick your ass up between your shoulders. You been told more than once. You could give the crew the shits."

"It's so damn hot it's burning my hands, Red," Barnes replied.

Rankin laughed out load. At least we'll know his hands are clean now."

"Just a reminder, Robishaw," Corbett interrupted. "We have a qual appointment at 1800 after we get in port to walk through the control room AC distribution system. Are you ready? If not don't waste my time. I have a lot to do and not too much time to do it while we are in Souda Bay."

"I'm ready," Robishaw replied. "I have a question. Where is Sevastopol? Never heard of it."

"It's about 1,500 miles from our current position in Ukraine on the Black Sea," Rankin replied. "I just made up our movement report to ComSixthFleet. We'll be on station in about three days give or take."

"Sure wish we could pull some liberty in Souda Bay. Fell in love with a beautiful Greek girl there once upon a time," Corbett remarked with a smile.

Chief Burgess entered the cress mess. "Barnes, I have good news. Your mess cooking assignment has been extended until we get back to home port in Norfolk."

"Damn COB. What did I do?" Barnes asked with a total defeated look.

"Nothing, Barnes. Since you are doing such a great job, I thought that we'd just keep you on for a while."

"No shit! Tell me that you're just kidding me. Red said that I was the worst mess cook ever."

Red stuck his head out from the galley. "You can say that again. He is the worst ever. Lost two perfectly good shit cans over the side. Doesn't know how to wash dishes."

Chief Burgess laughed. "No. But really, Jones and Peterson were scheduled to relieve you, but we just got word that they made third class from the last exams. So, It's your turn in the barrel again."

"Now prepare to surface. Station the maneuvering watch," came over the general announcing system.

Chief Burgess and Rankin hurried up the ladder back to the control room. The other crew members quickly left for their assigned stations for entering port.

Chief Sullivan and Corbet were on watch in maneuvering along with Johnson on the electrical panel and Franklin on reactor control.

Kelly came into maneuvering and stood looking at Johnson for a moment. "Cricket, I thought I told you to keep your ass out the ELT lab. There was a plastic bag on the counter that is missing. You get it?"

"Yeah, I did. Sorry, Kelly but I really needed it."

"You really screwed up and I mean big time, Cricket," Kelly continued. "I had just used that plastic bag for a sample. It's probably contaminated. I have to confiscate your teeth, Cricket."

"No shit. You're kidding me. Right, Kelly? This must be some kind of joke."

"Give me the damn bag and we can check it out," Kelly replied.

Johnson took the bag containing his teeth from its usual spot on top of the electrical panel and accompanied Kelly to the ELT lab.

In the ELT lab Kelly placed the bag with the teeth in the Pig, closed the door and turned it on. A loud crackling sound came from the instrumentation as the meter reading pegged indicating a very high level of radioactive contamination.

"That's it. Sorry, Cricket. Like I said, I have to confiscate your teeth for decontamination," Kelly said with a stern look.

"So when can I have my teeth back? Can't eat without them you know?".

"Not sure, buddy. Depends on what type of contamination it is. I actually might have to grind them up and then discharge them overboard. Should know in a few days maybe a week," Kelly replied with a tone of uncertainty in his voice. "Sorry, Cricket but I warned you."

With a totally defeated look, Petty Officer Johnson turned and left the lab to resume his watch. As he entered maneuvering, Corbett asked, "How did it go, buddy? Get your teeth back?"

Johnson replied, "Don't want to talk about it."

What Johnson didn't know was that before bringing his confiscated teeth to the lab, Kelly had careful placed a test sample of radioactive material in the Pig. Johnson's teeth were in fact clean as could be. Kelly had not yet decided how long he would keep the teeth.

While moored at the NATO base in the port of Souda Bay, the most time-consuming tasks would be loading additional stores aboard to feed a crew of over hundred men for six months. Red and his mess cooks would be working for many hours with help from all departments on the boat. A task just as important to many would be swapping the movies onboard for new ones. The person in charge of the movie detail would get holy hell if many of the new movies were not new releases.

Chief Burgess entered the crews mess and asked in a stern voice, "Anyone seen Doc? I've looked everywhere for him. I have his supplies that need to be stowed away."

"I was on topside watch earlier when he left the boat, Chief," Snell replied. "I saw him going up the pier just after we docked. Didn't see where he went."

"No one is supposed to leave the boat," the chief said with a concerned look. "Did he say where he was going?"

"I asked but he just said that he had to pick up some medical supplies and that he would not be gone long. Am I in trouble, Chief? Not sure what I was supposed to do."

Chief Burgess replied, "Since you're here, Snell, go with Franklin on the movie run. Pick up the Jeep at the guard station at the head of the pier. You still have your military driver's license, don't you?"

"Yeah, Chief but darn it! I just got off watch. Why me?"

"Yours is not to ask why. Just do it, Sailor," the chief replied.

"Well damn it, if anyone sees Doc, tell him that I am looking for him. If what I am thinking is true, his ass is in a sling," the chief remarked as he left to continue his search.

"Kline...report topside... Doc Kline... report topside to the COB ASAP," blared over the general announcing system.

It was close to 2200 when the XO entered the Captain's stateroom. "Sorry, Captain but we have a major problem."

The captain slowly got up and sat on the edge of his bunk. "What's the problem, Leonard?"

"There's been an accident. Petty Officer Franklin and Seaman Snell were returning from a movie run. The Jeep they were riding in ran off the road into a ditch. Franklin was driving. It was dark and he was obviously not familiar with the area. Unfortunately, Seaman Snell was killed. The police report states that Franklin had alcohol on his breath. He is in custody at the local police station. The body was taken to the local hospital."

Captain Flynn got dressed as quickly as he could. He paced back and forth in his stateroom for several minutes before he spoke. "Alright XO, this is what I want you to do. Conjure up all your JAG skills and conduct a formal investigation of the accident as quickly as you can. I want it in my hands in three hours at the most. I will contact the local embassy to have them take custody of Franklin from the police and bring him back here. Get the word to Franklin to keep his mouth shut and make no statements to anyone. After transmitting it to ComSixthFleet and ComSubLant, we will have the investigation report delivered to the local magistrate and the embassy. After Franklin is back onboard, the embassy duty officer and I will work to complete all the paperwork necessary to get Seaman Snell's body prepared and onboard the first available flight back to the states. I will check with the embassy and customs, but I believe they will also need a passport for the body. I will also contact a retired Army colonel I know that lives near here. He was liaison officer with NATO and has handled the transfer of many deceased soldiers state side. He is a long-time friend of mine and I am sure he will help. We don't have much time. We will get underway on schedule."

"How about Franklin? He will be ordered to remain in the country until a court convenes to hear the charges against him."

"That's where you come in, Leonard. In the investigation you will determine that without a doubt Seaman Snell was the driver when it went into that ditch. Is that clear?"

"But Captain, that..."

"Don't worry, Leonard. Before we reach Norfolk, I will submit an amended investigation stating that further investigation revealed that Franklin was the driver. Local Norfolk authorities and the Navy JAG Corp will take it from there and administer justice. I will prepare the letter to Seaman Snell's next of kin as soon as possible expressing regrets for their terrible loss. Seaman Snell's death was tragic, but no crew member of mine is going to spend the rest of his life in a Greek prison. Not if there's anything I can do about it."

Before daylight (***Redacted***) stationed the maneuvering watch in preparation for getting underway. The executive officer proceeded to the bridge and reported to the captain. "All departments are ready to get underway. Franklin is on board and Seaman Snell is on his way home, Captain. Didn't think we could do it."

"Well done, Leonard," the captain remarked with a smile.

"There is another problem, Captain."

"What the hell is wrong now?" the captain asked.

"We are missing one man at muster. It's Doc Kline."

The captain lowered and shook his head in disbelief. "We have a third-class corpsman onboard, don't we?" the captain asked.

"Yes, we do, Captain. Petty Officer Ramsey," the XO replied.

"We sure as hell can't wait for Kline. Let's get underway," the captain ordered with a stern look. "XO notify the NATO Naval Support Activity, Souda Bay regarding our AWOL crewmember."

The *(Redacted)* steamed out into the harbor leading to the Sea of Crete headed for the deeper waters of the Mediterranean. The captain was on the bridge with the officer of the deck.

One of the lookouts on the bridge reported. "Sir, we have a contact bearing 180 degrees. It's closing fast on our stern."

The officer of the deck replied, "Very well, let me know immediately if the contact changes course."

"ECM/Sonar… this is the Captain. Can you identify that contact astern?"

"Capt'n... this is ECM. It has the electronic signal of a Soviet destroyer. I can't identify the hull number as yet. It appears that it quickly up anchored in the Souda Bay harbor to intercept us."

"Very well," the captain replied over the intercom.

"Radar… give me range, course and speed of the contact astern. Also, what is the projected closest point of approach (CPA)?" the captain ordered as he peered through his binoculars.

"Captain…radar, contact range 4,000 yards...course zero-two-zero degrees…speed 25 knots. She is steaming at flank speed. The CPA will be 500 yards on our port side."

"Very well," the captain acknowledged. "Let me know if there is any change."

"What are your orders Capt'n? Should I announce battle stations?" the officer of the deck asked.

"No, Barney. Just relax. Maintain your course and speed. We are too shallow to submerge right now," the captain replied. "We'll just let him catch up and see what his intentions are."

The lookout reported, "The contact is signaling us, Sir."

"Quartermaster…this is the Captain. Come to the bridge with the Aldis lamp and I hope you are up on your Morse code."

Rankin accompanied by a young quartermaster trainee carrying a note pad reached the bridge just as the contact reached its CPA on the port side. After a few moments Rankin reported, "They are signaling the International Code for… IDENTIFY YOURSELF…IDENTIFY YOURSELF. The signal flag instructions at the mast are directing us to heave to for a search."

The captain stood silent as the Soviet destroyer repeated the order several more times.

"Captain… this is ECM. The contact has just announced Battle Stations."

"Very well ECM. Was that announcement in Russian or Ukrainian?"

"Not sure, Captain…the best I can make out…it's…Polish. The ship's electronic and sonar pattern is consistent with the ORP Wodnik (251). Designated a training ship, Captain. Home port is listed as Gdynia, Poland on the Baltic."

The destroyer sent the order again,

IDENTIFY YOURSELF…IDENTIFY YOURSELF

The captain shook his head, smiled and ordered, "Quartermaster… reply to the contact, WE ARE A SUBMARINE…WE ARE A SUBMARINE."

Rankin sent the reply with a huge smile.

The captain directed the officer of the deck, "Barney….right full rudder…increase speed to 30 knots…make your course one-six-zero."

"Aye, aye, Captain," he replied.

(Redacted) turned to starboard and quickly opened the range to the contact. After a few moments, the destroyer ORP Wodnik (251) slowly turned in the opposite direction back toward Crete.

The captain turned to the officer of the deck. "Barney, I'm going below. I'll be in my stateroom. Don't hesitate to call me when in doubt. The navigator will inform you when you can submerge in accordance with my night orders."

"Aye, aye, Captain. Should we send an Incident Report to ComSixFleet notifying them that we have been detected and identified by the Soviet fleet?" the officer the deck asked.

"Negative, Barney. The destroyer was not equipped with advanced sonar or ECM equipment. I would venture to say that all they know now is we are a submarine and with no known nationality."

"I understand," the officer of the deck replied as the captain turned and hurried down the bridge hatch to the control room below.

One of the lookouts on the bridge laughed out loud for a few moments while everyone else on the bridge remained silent. "What in the hell was all that about?" he mumbled to himself.

The XO knocked on the captain's stateroom door and entered. "Captain, we just received a message from NATO headquarters in Souda Bay. They have Petty Officer Kline. There're asking what you would like to do with him."

"Well, what the hell, XO? What are our alternatives for Christ sake?" the captain responded with a tone of utter disgust, anger and uncertainty. It was obvious that this situation was the last thing he wanted to deal with now.

"They can send him under custody to ComSixthFleet in Naples, or they can just transfer him back to us by helicopter if we are can arrange a rendezvous. I recommend we try to get him back onboard, Captain."

"You handle this situation, XO. Talk to the navigator and see if we can rendezvous before we submerge. If we can, then do it! If not, they can just ship his sorry ass off to Naples. Keep me informed." Although extremely angry, Captain Flynn was also very relieved that Doc had been located.

It was learned later that several members of the crew did what they could to give the helicopter carrying their shipmate Doc Kline a little extra time to reach the boat before it was scheduled to submerge. In maneuvering Chief Sullivan without authority reduced speed by a couple of knots which went unnoticed. On the helm, Wallace intentionally let the boat's heading drift off a direct course and steered with a slight zigzag which increased the distance to travel. Quartermaster Rankin would never discuss what he did to help. He was, however, responsible for monitoring the fathometer and tracking the depth of water below the keel to determine the appropriate point to submerge the boat. The truth be known...*(Redacted)* could have safely submerged a little sooner.

The helicopter managed to reach *(Redacted)* and transfer DOC Kline by rescue hoist a mere ten minutes before the boat was scheduled to submerge. Based upon what was told by the COB and men topside that assisted in the transfer, Doc Kline's dress white uniform was heavily soiled and covered with lipstick. He had on socks with no shoes, white hat, belt or sailor knot necktie. He smelled like he had bathed in the Greek liquor Ouzo. The helicopter missed its first attempt to transfer its passenger. Doc Kline bounced off the side of the boat and skimmed across the water before reaching the safety of the deck of the boat.

The captain quickly convened a Commanding Officer's Non-Judicial Punishment hearing. Petty Officer First Class Kline pleaded guilty to the charge of AWOL and was reduced in rank one stripe to petty officer second class and fined half pay for six months. He was placed on restriction and could not leave the boat for three months. The restriction did not mean much at all since the boat would be at sea much longer than his restriction. Some would say that Doc got off light. Missing ship movement is a more serious offense than just AWOL. An additional charge of being out of uniform added by the XO was dismissed.

When asked if it was worth it, Doc thought for a moment and answered with a laugh, "Damn straight! I'd give up another stripe for just one more night ashore."

Later that day the navigator knocked, entered the captain's stateroom and laid out the navigation charts on the captain's table. "Captain, I would like to discuss our movement report from the Sea of Crete to Sevastopol. The depth of the Bosporus Strait is 200 feet at its deepest depth and the merchant ship traffic is extremely heavy. It's the same with the Strait of the Dardanelles. I recommend that we transit through the Bosporus and Dardanelles mid channel at a depth of 100 feet, speed 20 knots. We should be able to navigate satisfactorily using the fathometer. Channel should be clear all the way."

"I understand your recommendation, George, but our latest intel report indicates that the Soviets have sonar arrays along the straits. As you know, our orders state that we must remain undetected in the Black Sea. I don't want to take that risk. We will transit at periscope depth. The heavy surface traffic in the straits should mask our pattern. You, the XO and I will rotate the watch in control on the periscope."

"I understand, Capt'n. I'll modify our movement report," he stated with a slight sigh of disappointment as he left the stateroom. He knew his assigned duties had just increased significant. He spent most of his free time eating and sleeping. He now has less of both.

The Navigator, Lieutenant Commander George Temple is a tall man, very thin in his early thirties, with dark hair and wears dark horned rimmed glasses. He is very intelligent and was selected for lieutenant commander a year early. As *(Redacted)*'s third officer and navigator, he has enormous responsibility for a man of his age. He is very capable and had on one occasion assumed command at sea. His position as navigator requires him to work long hours. He is often on his feet for at least sixteen hours. His turn on watch at the periscope extends his day with only four hours sleep.

After only a few hours sleep, it was the navigator's turn to be on watch in the control room. He tried to get out of his bunk but fell back with pain in his legs. He lay still for a moment staring at the overhead. "Damn it," he remarked as he picked up the intercom microphone. "Control this is the navigator. Please have Doc Kline come to my stateroom."

Kline entered the navigator's stateroom. "You asked for me, Mr. Temple? What seems to be the problem?"

"Hey Doc, Glad to see that you're back aboard," the navigator remarked with a big smile. "It's my legs…feet."

Kline pulled back his cover on his bunk. Mister Temple's legs were swollen, and his feet were twice the normal size. "You have a severe case of edema. You'll have to stay off your feet in your bunk for the next several days. I'll tell the Stewart to eliminate salt in your meals. I'll also put you on a diuretic."

"That's not possible, Doc. No way I'm going to lay flat on my ass for that long," he replied.

"Those are my orders. I'll talk to the XO. Maybe you'll listen to him," he replied as he left the stateroom.

In a few minutes the XO entered the room. "George... Doc explained the situation to me. I talked to the captain. You are relieved as navigator. I'll assume your responsibilities for a few days, and we'll see how you are doing."

"I guess I have no choice. I stand relieved, Sir," he remarked as the XO left the stateroom.

The navigator's condition was not unusual among the crew of *(Redacted)* as well as many other medical problems. The long hours on watch and other duties took a toll on many during the time at sea during deployments. The extra duties associated with special operations made the situation even more severe.

Deployment- 142 Days

The date was 24 September 1967. *(Redacted)* reached its destination on the Black Sea and in the weeks and months that followed, *(Redacted)* detected and charted the early warning radar systems and communications from the Soviet base. The crew celebrated Thanksgiving, Christmas and New Years without family and friends by their side which was not an unusual circumstance for this crew and many others around the world. Holidays were just another routine day at sea. Turkey and cranberry sauce were the evening meal on Thanksgiving. By Christmas baked canned ham was the specialty since food stores were starting to be depleted. Fresh eggs and milk were quickly replaced by cardboard powered substitutes. Shit-on-a shingle was the staple for breakfast. Liver and onions were in great supply since that was the captain's favorite meal.

Unlike the crew's mess, meals in the officer's wardroom were more formal. No one start eating until the captain was seated. No one left the table before the captain unless they were excused.

The evening meal was often reserved for compliments or reprimands to junior officers from the captain.

The commissary officer was often chastised by the captain during dinner in the wardroom because the liver was not prepared properly. He explained to the commissary officer in detail the proper way to cook liver and expected him to relay his directions to the cook. The young junior officer, however, did not dare discuss again the proper way to prepare liver with Red the cook. He was told by Red on more than one occasion, "respectfully…go shove it up your ass…Sir." The young commissary officer was deeply indebted to Red since he always kept the food consumption and reports within budget. Red was an expert at creative accounting. Many junior officers were often relieved of duty and given an unsatisfactory fitness report for the serious offense of going over the allotted food budget. The sought-after prize Battle Efficiency Award E was often lost by boats because of commissary budget overruns. Such were the pitfalls of a naval officer career during peace time which was often an undeclared conflict with the Soviet Union.

During these many months the boat remained undetected and its mission proceeded without incident. The commanding officer's most desired prey, however, had eluded him. A test of a surface to surface missile had not been tracked and photographed. He didn't have long to wait.

Deployment-246 Days

The date is 6 January 1968. In his stateroom, the captain was reading the following message announcement:

In Geneva, the International Red Cross *announced that Israel and Egypt had agreed to conditions for releasing the prisoners of war who had been captured in June during the Six-Day-War. At the time, there were 4,000 Egyptian POWs and only 20 Israeli ones to be exchanged, in that agreements had already been worked out with Jordan, Syria, Lebanon and Iraq.*

"Nothing was mentioned about the two Seal Team Charlie members that I heard were captured. Not surprising," the captain muttered to himself.

"Captain to control…Captain to control!" the officer of the deck called on the intercom. "Fire control radar detected; evaluated possible pre-firing operation."

"I have something here on the ECM scope, Sir," the spec ops electronics technician on watch reported to the officer of the deck in control. "I'm not sure, but… Yes, it is a Russian type Lima Two Tango fire control radar; classified missile tracking, Sir."

The captain hurried to the control room and took position at the periscope. "Station the photo recon party. Let's don't miss this one. We may not get another chance."

A report came over the intercom from the communications center. "Captain, this is radio, we just picked up encrypted voice communications from the test range near the Soviet naval base. Missile firing in five minutes."

"Excellent! Get the periscope camera in position. I'll take the photographs myself," the captain said excitedly.

"Sonar contact, Sir," came suddenly over the intercom from the sonar room. "Bearing three-zero-five…range 10,000 yards, turn count one-nine-five…classified destroyer escort."

The captain swung the periscope to the reported bearing and switched to high power.

"Damn it!" he shouted. "Destroyer, closing fast, man battle stations torpedo."

"Now, man battle stations, torpedo." blared over the announcing system.

The sailors jumped quickly out of their bunks and crowded into the passageways as they hurried to their assigned stations. In 50 seconds, battle stations were manned in all compartments.

The chief of the watch in control reported to the captain, "Battle stations manned, Sir."

"Very well," the captain acknowledged. "Make all torpedo tubes ready in all respects. Report course and speed of the contact, compute estimated time of arrival and CPA."

The executive officer, as fire control supervisor, coordinated the actions of the fine control party as they fed data received over the intercom communications system into the computer.

"Control...sonar, contact will pass across our port quarter at a range of 2,000 yards...bearing one-five-zero...speed 10 knots."

"He's echo ranging on his sonar now, Capt'n," the executive officer reported.

"Very well...standby," the captain replied. "We've lots of time. Missile firing in one minute."

The executive officer paced back and forth in front of the periscope station as the seconds slowly ticked away. "I think we should go deep, Capt'n. That destroyer could pick us up any time now," he remarked nervously.

The captain remained silent as he swung around the periscope.

"Echo ranging time has doubled, Capt'n. He has contact. Speed increased to 25 knots," the sonarman reported.

At the same time ECM reported, "Missile away, Capt'n!"

"I have it in sight," he said as he adjusted the focus on the periscope and slid the camera in place. He worked quickly and expertly as he operated the shutter on the camera and adjusted the periscope to follow the missile in flight.

"ECM...this is the Captain. Are you receiving the fire control data from the missile?"

"That's affirmative, Captain. Signals are loud and clear."

"The lighting conditions couldn't be better. Should be some fine pictures, fine as wine," the captain remarked almost casually.

"Contact range 6,000 yards...closing fast," sonar reported.

"Very well," the captain acknowledged.

The executive officer stood rigid and stared at the target range indicator on the computer as the range became smaller and smaller. "What is he trying to do? We should get the hell out of here or shoot before he starts depth charging us," he mumbled in a low voice.

"Contact range 4,000 yards," sonar again reported.

"Very well," the captain acknowledged. "A few more seconds is all I need." He snapped the shutter for the last photograph and smiled, "Yes, that should be a fine one. Right on the..."

The executive officer jerked his head around from the computer. "Fire one! Aye, Sir," he said as he pressed the firing key.

"No!" the captain shouted as he jumped from the periscope station and struck the officer with a devastating body blow. The blow sent the executive officer slamming against the opposite bulkhead, temporarily unconscious. The captain's efforts were to no avail.

"Torpedo away; running hot, straight and normal," sonar reported.

"Oh my God," the captain said very slowly. "How good was your fire control solution?" he asked.

"The best," the computer operator reported with a thumbs up.

"Why do you have to be so damn good?" he remarked as he returned to the periscope station.

"I hope that destroyer changes course pretty damn quick. Lower the periscope. Take her deep, ahead full, right full rudder!"

The submarine banked to starboard sharply and took a steep down angle as the speed increased. In a few seconds, she had reached the safety of the deep.

"Twenty seconds until detonation," the computer operator reported.

The seconds passed slowly. Everyone in the control room stood absolutely still and no one spoke a word in anxious anticipation. The silence was suddenly broken by a distant muffled explosion. The submarine shook slightly from the shock wave, and the lights dimmed momentarily. A roar of cheers came from the men in the control room.

"Knock it off, damn it!" the captain shouted.

Everyone froze in their positions. It became deathly quiet as they watched the captain lower his head to his forearm braced against the bulkhead. He ran his hand through his streaked gray hair.

Suddenly over the intercom "Capt'n…sonar, we have another contact bearing zero-nine-zero degrees…range 10,000 yards closing fast. It is another destroyer."

"Ahead full, make your depth eight-zero-zero feet, right full rudder, steady on course one eight zero degrees," the captain ordered.

"Capt'n…sonar, two splashes range 8,000 yards. Designated depth charges."

The captain hurriedly passed over the general announcing system, "All compartments rig for depth charge. Close all unnecessary sea valves. Damage control party man your stations." *A stream of sweat rolled down his face. "Appears they panicked and dropped too soon. Hope to hell that's true," he thought to himself.*

A muffled explosion could be heard in the distance and then another in quick succession. The (**Redacted**) shook as the mild shockwave hit. The compartment lights flickered several times.

"Capt'n… sonar, multiple splashes…range 3,000 yards; heavy cavitation; designated destroyer escort closing fast off our starboard side. Light cruiser detected…range 10,000 yards. They have us boxed in, Captain."

"Ahead flank, make your depth one-zero-zero-zero feet, left full rudder, steady on course two-seven-zero degrees," the captain ordered as he paced back forth.

Four explosions rocked the *(Redacted)* violently from side to side before settling back to the upright position. The boat slowed from her rapid decent as the lighting went out. Emergency lights dimly lit up the various compartments.

"Capt'n…maneuvering, reactor scram…steam turbine shutdown and shifting to emergency battery power. Making minimum turns."

The lighting throughout the boat returned to normal on battery power.

"Maneuvering this is the Captain. Get the reactor back to power as quickly as possible. As soon as you have steam, bring the plant back online. You have my permission to bypass all safety features to get back to power. When you have power, start up and engage the RPJ propulsion system."

"Diving officer continue to a depth of one-two- zero-zero feet," the captain ordered in a calm quiet voice. "If we can't outrun those son-of- a-bitches, we'll see if we can hide."

(Redacted) proceeded slowly to a depth of 1,200 feet. The hull of the submarine creaked and made strange indescribable noises as the ocean pressure increased on the metal hull. The submarine was far below its designed depth and near what should have been crush depth.

"She held together before at this depth. Let's see if she can do it again," the captain remarked as he slowly paced back and forth at the periscope station.

"All compartments rig for silent running and report damages to control," continued over the announcing system.

"Capt'n...sonar, we have multiple splashes close aboard. Depth charge clicks indicate deep depth settings."

The explosions again rocked the *(Redacted)* violently from side to side before settling back to the upright position as the boat again went dark. The breakers supplying power from the emergency battery tripped and all electrical systems on board went offline. Only the small emergency lights dimly lit the disabled submarine.

"We're dead in the water, Captain," the chief of the watch in the control room reported. "All systems down."

"Contact all compartments, Chief. Make sure that sound power phones are manned," the captain ordered. "I want communications established and I want it done now."

"Aye, aye, Captain," the chief of the watch replied. "Sound powered phones manned in all compartments, Sir."

"Very well. Diving officer, hover in place and maintain your current depth," the captain ordered. "Contact the engineering officer. I want power from the emergency batteries restored and now!"

"Mister Eddy reports that he has men working to restore power. Should have battery power soon, Captain," the chief of the watch explained.

In the control room, the men worked to maintain depth with no power the best they could. High pressure air was blown slowly into the ballast tanks to decease depth and then flooded to increase depth.

"Capt'n...sonar, all systems down. Our last contact appeared to be multiple splashes overhead. Depth settings unknown."

The men in control waited in anxious anticipation for the explosions that were sure to come…and they did!

(***Redacted***) shook violently as the shock waves from each of the six depth charges hit one after the other. One seemed more violent than the one before and the impact sent the boat heeling over to starboard at a 60-degree angle. It hovered over at the excessive angle for what seemed like an eternity to the men aboard (***Redacted***) before it settled back to an upright position. The explosions forced the boat drifting downward to a deeper and dangerous depth.

"Depth is 1,500 feet, Captain," the diving officer reported.

"Blow all main ballasts, Chief!" the captain ordered. "Cycle the forward tank vents to keep the angle off and open all vents when we reach one-zero-zero-zero feet! If we get hit again at this depth, it'll blow us apart."

"Blowing all ballast tanks. Standing by to cycle the forward vents!" the chief of the watch reported as the submarine moved slowly upward.

"Try to keep that zero angle the best you can diving officer," the captain ordered.

"Aye, aye, Captain," the diving officer replied.

"At one-zero-zero-zero feet and all ballast tank vents open, Sir," the chief of the watch reported.

Several faint explosions were heard in the distance.

"Looks like they've lost contact," the captain said in soft voice.

The captain could no longer control his frustration which had been slowly building. "A damn multimillion-dollar submarine and we were put out of action by a few depth charges! Those depth charge attack studies against high tech computerized modern submarines are a bunch of crap!" he shouted in a loud voice which surprised everyone in control. "They can jam those computer simulated depth charge attacks up their ass as far as I'm concerned. I would be more than happy to do it for them!"

He was able to calm his anger as he paced back and forth at the periscope station. With an unexpected grin, he remarked, "I would have traded this boat for a less complicated fleet diesel boat a few minutes ago."

Faint bouts of unexpected laughter also followed from the men on watch in the control room.

The captain remarked with a big grin, "Don't tell anyone I said that guys. Okay?"

The lights in the compartments suddenly came on.

"Control...maneuvering, battery power is restored, making minimum turns, bringing the reactor to power."

"Capt'n...sonar, I have three contacts at 6,000 yards range opening. It appears they're setting up a search sector. Active sonar pings from the destroyer escorts. Don't anticipate that the sonar will penetrate the thermal layer at approximately 1,000 feet."

"Sonar...this is the Captain. Very well! Well done! Keep me informed of any closing contacts."

"Control...engine room, flooding in the lower level," came over the intercom. The worst fears of a submarine crew were about to come true. Sea water entered the engine room through a ruptured condenser cooling sea water pipe. At that depth the enormous volume of water was rapidly filling the lower level of the engine room. The crew in the engine room had only minutes before the compartment was totally flooded and the boat would be unable to recover before heading to the ocean bottom.

"Sound the collision alarm! Check all watertight doors closed and dogged!" the captain ordered. "Blow all main ballast tanks. Make your depth one-zero-zero feet. Have to reduce the sea pressure and give the guys more time in the engine room to stop that flooding. Open the vents at one-zero-zero feet, Chief"

"Depth one-zero-zero feet, aye, Sir," replied the diving officer. "Make your depth one-zero- zero feet smartly," he passed to the planesman.

Like an aircraft pilot the planesman pulled back on his depth control stick as the boat angled up to reach the safety of shallow water. The chief of the watch opened the main ballast tank vents at 100 feet to slow the accent.

"Depth is one-zero-zero feet, Sir," the diving officer reported as he leveled the boat off at the ordered depth.

Machinist Mate White was on watch in the engine room. He quickly climbed down the ladder to the lower level and wadded into the waist deep water in the flooding bilge to reach the sea water steam condenser system. He struggled against the gushing torrent of incoming seawater to reach the isolation valve. The force of the seawater knocked him backward several times before he finally reached the valve. As he struggled and turned the isolation valve, the incoming seawater slowly stopped.

"Control... engine room, flooding in the lower level is under control. Emergency bilge pump is online. Pumping bilges to sea. Bilge level is decreasing," came over the intercom.

"Very well...well done engineering," the captain replied. "Sonar...this is the Captain. We are above the thermal layer. Let me know if it appears that we have been detected by any surface ships."

"Aye, aye, Capt'n, I hear echo ranging in the distance. Recommend we remain at silent running for a while longer. The surface ships will definitely pick up the cavitation noise from our direct drive propulsion."

"Very well sonar. That is my intention at this time," replied the captain.

"Control...this is maneuvering, reactor at 20 percent power, steam generators are at minimum pressure, bringing on steam to the RPJ propulsion system."

"Very well maneuvering. Shift from battery power to RPJ."

"Helm make turns for 12 knots," the captain passed to the helmsman. He stood leaning on the periscope with his head down resting on his forearm.

After a few moments, he quickly raised his head and spoke to the young officer beside him, "Barney, you have the conn. Make your course one-eight-zero. Remain at this depth. Secure from battle stations. I'm going to my stateroom. Don't hesitate to call me when in doubt."

"Aye, aye, Captain," the officer of the deck replied softly.

The captain slowly walked to the ladder leading below, stopped and turned, "Well done men. Well done," he said with some difficulty and disappeared down the hatch.

Low chatter commenced among the men in the control room.

"I wouldn't want to be in the XO's shoes."

"They'll hang him from the highest tree."

The executive officer pulled himself up from the deck where he'd been lying for many minutes. He dusted his clothes and looked around the room.

The silence was again evident as everyone stared at him. He took off the headset of the phone he was wearing and let them fall to the deck. "I told him we should go deep."

It was a standoff for a few moments before the silence was broken by an unknown voice.

"Don't worry Mister Little. You're safe now."

"Our Hero."

"The sky is falling Chicken Little."

"Who said that?" the XO asked. "That's insubordination. I'll put you all on report. I can do it. You know I can."

Silence prevailed again. The executive officer quickly left the control room.

The captain sat with his head lowered to his folded arms on his desk. The executive officer suddenly burst into the stateroom and spoke desperately, "It wasn't my fault, Captain. I thought you said fire. The destroyer was closing fast, and I thought it was about to start depth charging. If you had broken off, when I recommended it, this would never have happened. You know…."

"Shut up!" the captain interrupted. "I think you fell apart out there, Leonard. We had plenty of time for evasion tactics. That destroyer would never have attacked until he had a positive submarine classification. You are fully aware of my standing orders. At battle stations you are to wait for my command, final bearing and shoot before you attack the target."

"Maybe we should go back and take a look. Maybe the destroyer was just damaged. There could be survivors. We can explain what happened. We can make them understand that it was..."

"I said, shut up. If you don't have anything intelligent to say, just don't say anything." The captain rose from his chair and approached the officer with clinched fist, forcing him against the bulkhead.

"We hit that ship with over a ton of TNT. There wouldn't be a splinter left big enough to pick your teeth with, much less survivors. This area will be swarming with more ships soon. Do you think I'm going up to them and announce who we are? I doubt if they'll be in a hand shaking mood." He fell back in his chair and sat in silence for a few moments. "Write up a message for transmission," the captain said slowly. "We'll have to make a report to the force commander immediately. After that, we'll let the politicians handle it."

"Right away, Captain. I'm sure everyone will agree that it was a mistake that could have happened to anyone."

The captain looked up with a stern expression. "If you say one more word to me except to acknowledge an order, I'll knock your teeth out." His expression softened. "You're the one that will have to live with the consequences. As commanding officer, I'm responsible for the deaths of the crew on the ship and I'll have to pay for it one way or another. Your responsibility in the incident will be determined at the court of inquiry when we reach port. You will have ample time to consider the possible outcome. I hope you can sleep nights. Now get out of my office."

The executive officer entered his stateroom, closed the door and sat at his desk. He looked at the various awards and commendations hanging on the bulkhead. He always thought of himself as an excellent officer and worked long and hard for his own command. He suddenly realized that when the chips were down, he didn't measure up; he was a coward. Standing up quickly, he ripped the plaques from the wall and threw them across the room.

The captain was lying on his bunk. He realized that he lost control during his reprimand of his executive officer. That was not a normal reaction during time of stress. His thoughts became incoherent as he stared at the overhead. Without moving his eyes from their fixed positions, he flipped the switch on the intercom beside him and spoke. "Navigator, this is the Captain. Make up our movement report and send it directly to the Naval Communications Center of the Force Commander. Take us home George. Mission accomplished."

"Will do, Capt'n," the navigator replied.

Chief Burgess (COB) knocked on the captain's door and entered. "Damage report, Captain."

"Yes, Chief," the captain replied. "What is our status?"

"We have 12 men injured. None are critical. Doc says nothing he can't handle. What could be some minor fractures. No need for emergency transfers. Torpedo tubes one and three are out of commission. The outer doors appear to be jammed. Engineering reports no major damage. Some equipment flooded in the engine room. Repairs are underway. A few packing gland and hull penetration leaks. Repairs are going well. Several main and auxiliary power motor driven breakers are out. They can be operated locally in manual. Engineer does not have an estimated time for these repairs. Repair parts could be an issue. Follow up report to follow."

"Very well, Chief. Did you give this report to the XO first?"

"Mister Little said that he did not want to be disturbed, Captain."

"Chief, you have my permission to tell the XO to snap out of it and get his ass in gear. We have a boat to run and we need his help to get back home. Is that clear?"

"It will be my pleasure, Captain," the COB replied with a smile as he left the stateroom.

SitRep 3-Fate Plays a Part

It was midnight. In the Commander Submarine Force Atlantic Fleet Communications Center, teletypes were beating out messages received from all parts of the world. Men in uniform hurried back and forth across the large room sorting and distributing message printouts. In the corner of the room, the communications duty officer sat at his desk and supervised the operation of the large complex. He had removed his coat and his collar was opened. The long hours were taking their toll on his eyes as he read through hundreds of messages which came across his desk. Empty paper coffee cups littered the floor around his trash can. The ashtray on his desk was full and spilled over to the papers.

A radioman approached the officer and handed him a message to be released. "Notice to Mariners Number 214, Sir, to be broadcast to all ships."

"What is it?"

"An oceanographic vessel has discovered an uncharted submerged mountain range, shallow sounding of 500 feet."

"What is its location?"

"Area Alpha Three, Point Juliet Tango. That would place it somewhere in this area here just south east of the Azores," the radioman said pointing to the large map on the wall.

"Any submarines transiting that area?" the officer asked.

"No, Sir," he answered.

The officer stamped and signed the message. "Assign it a precedence of routine. Broadcast it after all the higher priority messages. Keep me informed on all changes to movements into that area."

"Aye, aye, Sir," the radioman acknowledged as he returned to his teletype. He filed the Notice to Mariners at the bottom of the stack of messages on his desk.

After a few minutes another radioman stood up from his teletype, ripped off the printout and hurried to the officer's desk. "Sir, I've just received a coded, top secret, flash message from NJYA, code name Superman. You'll have to decode it."

The officer pulled a folder from his desk and quickly peered down the column of names. "*(Redacted)*," he mumbled.

"What was that?" the radioman asked.

The officer stood up quickly, "Nothing," he said as he hurried to the decoding room. He proceeded to decode the message.

TOP SECRET

FLASH

FROM: USS **(Redacted)** (*SSN- HULL NUMBER CLASSIFIED*) NYJA

TO: COMSUBLANT

CODE NAME: SUPERMAN

1. MISSION COMPLETED. RETURNING TO PORT AT BEST SPEED.

2. SOVIET DESTROYER ENGAGED AND SUNK IN INTERNATIONAL WATERS. EVADED OTHER ATTACKING VESSELS. INCURRED MINIMAL DAMAGE.

3. STATUS OF PROPULSION SYSTEM AND SONAR PATTERN DETECTION UNKNOWN.

4. MOVEMENT REPORT TO FOLLOW.

"Good God Almighty," the officer gasped. Grabbing his briefcase and the message, he hurried back to the message center. "Call upstairs and get my relief down here right away," he said to the radioman. "I have to get this message hand delivered to the deputy commander right away."

"Is it that hot?" the radioman asked.

"It's more than that," he answered as he hurried out the door to the parking lot. He got in his car and sped away quickly for the 15-mile drive across town.

"Didn't even give me time to make a file copy," the radioman commented to himself as he shook his head. "I'm going to be in the deep shits over this," he remarked as he returned to his teletype.

The traffic was heavy, and it seemed like every traffic light was against him as he drove through the city. He felt relieved as he turned down the street which would take him directly to the expressway. From there, it would be easy sailing across the river to the senior officers' quarters where the deputy commander was staying. The final traffic light ahead turned yellow as he approached it. He pushed the accelerator to the floor hoping to get across before it turned red. He looked to his right and only caught a glimpse of the large truck just before it struck

The impact of the truck threw the small car high in the air and down an embankment. Over and over it rolled before it came to rest in a ditch. A white plume of smoke rose from the rear of the car. Suddenly, it exploded into flames.

Onboard the (***Redacted***) the navigator worked diligently with his quartermaster plotting the return course to port. "That does it," he sighed and threw his pencil on the chart table. "Write up the coordinates of that course and we'll get our movement report out to the ComSubLant."

"Will do, Mister Temple," Rankin acknowledged.

"You have the area cross reference. Could you call them out to me?"

Leafing through the navigational tables, Rankin stopped and read, "The areas are Alpha Two, Alpha Three and Bravo Four. From there it's a straight shot to port with fun and games with the baby's mother."

"That does it I guess," Rankin commented. "I'll add the transit depth of 350 feet which you ordered and a speed for this leg of 20 knots,"

"No, the Captain desires to remain deep on the return transit to make sure we are not detected," the navigator remarked.

"The thermal layer is at 350 feet, so make our depth 450 f… no, make that 500 feet. That will give us a measure of safety."

"What's the shallowest depth of water we should expect, Sir?" the quartermaster asked.

"Let's see now," The navigator said as he studied the chart. "All fathometer soundings should be in the ballpark of 3,000 feet. We're home safe. Write up the message and I'll get it to the captain for release."

The movement report was prepared in message form and approved by the captain.

"How's it going, Marconi?" the navigator asked as he entered the radio room.

"Very funny, Mister Temple," the radioman answered.

"I have an operational immediate message to send. I want it to go directly to the Force Commander Communications Center."

"Will do, Sir," he replied. "I have a broadcast coming in now. After I've copied it, I'll get your message out."

The navigator left the Radio Room and the radioman sat down at his teletype as it beat out the incoming messages:

ROUTINE

UNCLASSIFIED

FROM: COMSUBLANT

TO: ALL SHIPS

SUBJECT: NOTICE TO ALL MARINERS NUMBER 214

1. SUBMERGED MOUNTAIN PEAK. SHALLOW DEPTH 500 FEET.

LOCATION: AREA IL313…

The transmission ended as the teletype stopped suddenly. The radioman checked the power switch and it was in the on position. Smelling a strange odor, he turned just as a power supply control box burst into flames. Sparks were thrown across the room and the lights went out. Battery powered emergency lights came on, dimly lighting the radio room.

"Fire in radio… fire in radio," was quickly passed over the announcing system followed by the gong of the general alarm.

Corbett was on watch in engineering; He quickly ran to the power distribution panel and pulled the breakers for the radio room in the operations compartment.

The captain entered the control room. "Prepare to surface. Remain submerged until I order otherwise," he commanded.

The officer of the deck acknowledged, "Aye, aye, Sir. The fire has been isolated. Chief Sullivan is in radio and the engineer is on his way, Capt'n."

"Very well," he replied.

Corbett entered the smoke-filled radio room with an emergency breathing apparatus over his face. He found Sullivan pulling at the burned smoldering wires of the equipment power supply.

"You can take that damn thing off. The smoke isn't very bad," the chief snapped. "I wish I could say the same thing for this panel."

"How does it look?" Corbett asked.

"Bad enough," Sullivan replied. "The panel wiring is shot. There's hydraulic oil all over the damn place in here. What isn't burned is soaked with oil. The complete panel will have to be rewired."

"Looks like I've got a job cut out for me," Corbett remarked in a disgusting tone. "Where did that damn oil come from?"

"Let's see. There! A small drop of oil just ran down that pipe and dripped on the panel," Sullivan said. "It's coming from that isolation valve in the overhead. These damn radiomen should have noticed that. It must have been dripping since the depth charge attack. Damn cunts!"

"Easy Chief, I can see how it could be missed," Corbett assured him. "We'd better cut Mister Eddy in on the problem."

After (**Redacted**) secured from fire quarters, the engineer, navigator and the two electricians met with the captain in the wardroom.

"What's the story?" the captain asked.

"It's simple, Capt'n," Sullivan replied. "The power supply to the communication equipment in radio is burn out."

"How long will it take to repair it?" the captain asked.

The chief thought a few moments and answered, "Six, maybe seven days working around the clock."

"Why so long? You could build a whole new panel in that time."

"That's just about what we have to do, Capt'n. There's over a hundred lead wires in there that have to be rerun. Then there are the transformers that have to be replaced. I don't even know if we have all the replacement parts. We may have to find substitutes in other equipment panels."

"How about a jury rig for temporary power, Chief?" the captain asked.

The chief hesitated. "No, Sir. That would take just as long and there are a few encryption circuits and panels that could be compromised, if we tried that. Not something I would recommend."

"Okay," the captain said with a sigh. "I have the picture. Did we get the movement report message out, George?"

"No, Capt'n," the navigator replied. "We are transiting right now without force commander approval."

"What do you recommend?"

"I recommend we surface and wait. The force commander will issue a SUBMISS alert if he doesn't receive our movement report shortly."

The captain was quiet for a few moments as he studied the navigational chart on the table. "Our incident report has been received by now. I have a feeling that the force commander will want us back in port as soon as possible."

"Yes, Sir, I agree," the navigator commented. "We could pull into Naples and wait until we restore communications."

The captain took another look at the chart and made his decision. "We are still under orders to remain undetected and unidentified. Naples is not a viable alternative. We will remain submerged and transit at best speed through the Straits of Gibraltar, Alpha Two and Alpha Three. If we have not made the communication repairs by then, we can make contact with special operations personnel in the Azores or Canary Islands on the secure short-range emergency transmitter. They can relay our movement report and ETA Norfolk to ComSubLant."

"Aye, aye, Captain," the navigator replied and followed the men out of the wardroom.

(Redacted) steamed back through the Marara and Aegean Seas from the Black Sea into the Mediterranean. The crew was getting anxious since they knew they would soon be reunited with friends and family. Little did they know that their return home would be delayed yet again.

"Captain, this is the officer of the deck," came over the intercom. "I need you in control, Sir."

The captain quickly entered the control room. "What's up, Jim?"

"In accordance with your standing orders, Captain, I've executed Crazy Ivan every four hours to clear our baffles. We have a contact dead astern, classified Foxtrot Class Soviet submarine. The range is in excess of 20,000 yards. She doesn't seem to be closing. Just tracking us."

After a few moments, the officer of the deck asked, "Think we should go quiet and try to evade her, Captain?"

"No, I don't want to risk that they could get a sonar trace of the RPJ. Maintain your current depth and increase speed to 30 knots. We should be through the Straits of Gibraltar in a few hours. We'll see if we can catch a thermal layer in the Atlantic and lose her at that time."

The submarine *(Redacted)* continued its journey beneath sea to its rendezvous with fate.

Deployment- 254 Days

The date was 14 January 1968. It was Sunday. The evening meal was about to be served on the *(Redacted).* The crew was looking forward to being home soon. The captain sat in his stateroom where he had spent most of his time for the past few days. He had only a little more than a week to prepare his patrol report, which would not be easy.

The navigator knocked on the captain's stateroom door and entered. "Navigator with the 1800 position report, Captain. We are approximately fifty miles inside of area Alpha Three."

"Very well, George. How accurate is your fix?"

"Pretty good, Captain. We could be a few miles off. The navigation system and gyros are still settling out a little after that loss of power," the navigator answered.

"Very well, carry on," the captain responded.

The navigator stopped and turned on his way out the door. "I know you're worried, Capt'n and you certainly have reason to be. I know I'm speaking for the whole crew when I say, I hope things turn out okay for you."

"Thank you, George but there's not much chance of that," the captain replied with a sigh. "The least that can happen is that I'll lose my command. I love this boat, George. It's become a part of me."

"There's always hope, Capt'n. We're all pulling for you," the navigator explained.

"We'll see," the captain replied as he turned back toward his desk.

The navigator left for the control room to make another check of the navigation system.

In the crew's mess, Red Thomas was preparing the last remaining steaks on the grill. He reached down and picked up a long red hair from one of the few T-bones and dropped it on the deck as he adjusted the tall white hat on his head.

Sammy Klein was in on his bunk in the crew's quarters. He had just closed the book which he was reading to get a few moments sleep before dinner. He removed a flask of medical pure grain alcohol from his locker next to him and took a hefty drink before returning it back to the locker.

Chief Sneed sat on a box in the bow compartment, cleaning a 45-caliber pistol which was disassembled and scattered around him.

Petty Officer Corbett, Chief Sullivan and Lieutenant Eddy were in the engine room along with several men on watch or completing qualification training. Corbett had gone aft to locate a spare part. Chief Sullivan and Lieutenant Eddy were on watch, to be relieved soon by the oncoming watch.

The COB had just completed the assignment of underway watches and training drills for the transit. He would review it with the XO for his approval.

Seaman Apprentice Barnes was about to clear everyone from the crew's mess in order to clean up and prepare for the evening meal. He was glad to soon be relieved of his duties as mess cook. He had decided to study to be an electricians mate like Petty Officer Corbett. He respected him very much since he had gone out of his way many times to help him with his qualifications.

Back home in their new homeport of Norfolk on television, everyone was watching the final few minutes of Super Bowl 11 in Miami. The Packers were beating the Raiders 37 to 14.

The navigator stood in the control room checking the chart. He took out the file of Notices to Mariners. "Rankin, you haven't entered change number 214 yet. It's right here on the message board and it is not signed."

"First call to the evening meal for the relieving watch section. First call to the evening meal," came over the general announcing system.

"No, Sir, I haven't," Rankin replied. "It's not complete. We received it on the last broadcast before the fire. It's so jumbled I couldn't make it out. Sorry, Sir. I guess I should have showed it to you. I just forgot with all that has happened. I am behind on the Notice to Mariners."

"I understand. We are all tired, Rankin. Don't worry about it but check all the Notice to Mariners and let's get all the charts updated as soon as possible. It was a routine message so nothing to worry about. Make a note to have Notice to Mariners 214 sent again as soon as we regain communications," the navigator explained as he rested his chin in his hand with his elbow on the chart table. He stared at the incomplete message.

1.SUBMERGED MOUNTAIN PEAK. SHALLOW DEPTH. 500 FEET. LOCATION: AREA I.L. 313

"Let's see now," the navigator spoke quietly to himself. "If it shifted to upper case and there are five bits on the teletype to each letter sequence, that would make the numbers transpose into A-P-H-A. That's AREA: ALPHA." He laid the chart aside and walked to the intercom unit on the bulkhead.

"Captain, this is the navigator."

At the same time the quartermaster strained his eyes for a second look at the fathometer to make sure he wasn't making a mistake. "Mister Temple, you'd better take a look at this. I'm getting a yellow sounding alarm of 1500 feet below the keel. According to the chart, it shouldn't be less than…"

Neither of the two men was able to complete his report. The submarine struck the submerged mountain peak on the starboard side of the bow compartment at full speed. The glancing blow sent (*Redacted*) veering off to port with a 60-degree list to port. Men and equipment were thrown into the air like ragdolls smashing against the port bulkhead. The starboard torpedo tubes were torn from their welds in the pressure hull and pushed back into the bow compartment. A wall of green gushed into the compartment under tremendous pressure and flowed down the passageways like a swollen river.

"Collision forward!" the officer of the deck yelled as he held tight to the periscope. "Emergency surface! Blow all main ballast tanks! Ahead flank! Full rise on the diving planes!"

The boat took a large up angle as it headed for the safety of the surface. The siren sounded throughout the boat. The bow compartment filled with water, which quickly spilled over into the upper levels and the control room blocking open the watertight door. A sailor attempting to close the door leading to the control room was quickly swept away.

Captain John Flynn struggled but was only able to reach the ladder leading up to control. There he was hit by a downpour of water which engulfed him.

Executive Officer Leonard Little stepped out of radio into the control room. He realized that he may not make it through the hatch leading aft to engineering in time and made the supreme sacrifice. He quickly shut and dogged the watertight door just before he was smashed against the watertight door and bulkhead by the oncoming wall of death.

Seaman Wallace remained in his depth control seat pulling back on the control stick gritting his teeth with eyes closed long after the water had risen above his head. He died at his station.

The officer of the deck in the control room picked up the short-range UQC underwater telephone and began transmitting. "Mayday! Mayday! This is submarine (**Redacted**). We are flooding! We are..." Lieutenant Junior Grade Barney Pool was not able to complete his message which went unheard in the vastness of the ocean.

In the crew's mess Commissaryman Red Thomas looked at the wall of water rushing in his direction. His instant reaction not surprisingly was "Oh shit," and a laugh cut short.

Seaman Apprentice Barns attempted to climb the ladder from the crew's mess to a higher level but was overtaken and swept away by the raging river of water. The other members of the crew in the crew's mess suffered the same fate.

In maneuvering, Machinist Mate Don White threw open the throttle on the turbines in response to the flank speed order.

"Give her all she's got!" Chief Sullivan yelled "Keep that speed on!"

The flooded electrical panels and battery forward caused a short circuit which tripped all the breakers on the power board in maneuvering and the engine room. The lights went out and the control rods for the reactor were released, dropped to the bottom of the reactor, shutting down the reactor. The steam turbines, shaft and the propeller slowly coasted to a stop. As the forward compartments filled, the submarine slowly halted its upward momentum, turned bow down and headed for the ocean depths quickly picking up speed. In the dimly lit engine room, terrified men grasped anything within reach as they rode the stricken submarine to what must be certain death. Uncontrolled sporadic words came out of the darkness along with whimpers and muffled screams.

"Oh my God!"

"We've had it!"

The submarine hit the muddy ocean bottom at a tremendous speed. It slid a short distance, throwing metal and debris in all directions. The impact again hurled the men in the engine room and auxiliary machinery space through the air and slammed them against obstacles in the compartments. The boat and scattered objects slowly came to rest on the ocean floor as if photographed in slow motion. No more than two minutes after the *(Redacted)* struck the submerged mountain peak, she lies dying like a wounded whale 300 hundred fathoms below the surface; the bow compartment and operations compartment flooded.

The most dreaded nightmare of a submariner had happened to the crew of *(Redacted).* Their many hours of training to combat such a casualty were of little use. The catastrophic flooding was swift and caught them unaware. The realization of the inevitable came to each of them in as many ways. Of the 117 aboard, including 7 special operations personnel, 108 perished. Some died slowly, others quickly, but all bravely. In the isolated aft compartments in engineering, fate chose to save a few. The ordeal of their shipmates forward was over while theirs had just begun.

Part Two: Story of Survival

SitRep 4-Survival

A large fish quickly darted from the path of a huge boulder which rolled slowly down the submerged mountain and came to a rest in the valley below. An avalanche of mud slid down the slope like a mountain river and diminished to a trickle. The hull of the submarine *(Redacted)* continued to settle and shift on the muddy ocean bottom. Muffled explosions of containers and tanks collapsing under the tremendous sea pressure in the flooded forward compartments vibrated throughout the boat. In the dimly lit engineering compartments residual steam escaped from a broken pipe and hissed softly in the distance. Faint moans and whimpers could be heard coming from the darkness.

Corbett grabbed hold of a pipe and pulled himself up. His left arm throbbed with pain. He managed to find a battery powered emergency light and shined it around the compartment.

"Can anyone hear me?" he shouted.

"Here! Over here!" a voice replied.

Corbett shined the light in the direction of the voice. "Who's that? Is that you, White?" he asked as he moved forward, stumbled and nearly fell.

"Yeah it's me," White replied as he crawled from behind the steam turbine on the starboard side.

"Are you alright?" Corbett asked as he helped him to his feet.

"I think so. I hurt like hell all over."

Corbett shined the light in his face. Blood poured down the side of his head and covered his ear. Pulling out a cloth from his back-pocket Corbett said, "Here, you're bleeding. Put this on that cut."

"What happened?" White asked as he leaned against the bulkhead. "The last thing I remember, I was standing in the passageway. When I woke up, I was upside down outboard the turbine."

"I don't know. We must have hit something. I wouldn't have given you a plug nickel for our chances a few minutes ago."

"At least we're alive, that is I think we're alive," White remarked as he touched his head and looked at the blood on his finger.

"We're not out of the woods yet, not by any means," Corbett replied.

"Somebody help me!" a voice shouted in the distance.

Corbett and White made their way forward over the debris in the passageway. "There's another emergency light, get it," Corbett snapped. "Let's get some more damn light in here so we can see what we're doing."

"Give me a hand. I can't get this thing off me," the voice spoke again. In the forward starboard corner Lee was pinned under an electrical panel which had broken loose and fell forward.

Corbett took hold of the panel and pulled but couldn't budge it. "I'll have to get a chain fall. Just hold on, Lee."

"I guess I'll have to. It doesn't hurt very much but I'm not very comfortable, that's for sure."

"You're one lucky bastard," Corbett remarked. "White, get over here and give me a hand!"

"Just a minute," he shouted. "Chief Sullivan is over here and I… I think he's dead."

Corbett hesitated and lowered his head. Thoughts of the chief passed through his mind; He quickly discarded the thoughts and continued his search for a chain fall to help Lee. He attached the chainfall hoist to the panel and the overhead. The panel rose easily as he tugged at the chain. He grabbed Lee by the underarms and pulled him free.

"It's my leg," Lee said. "It hurts like blue blazes. I think it's broken."

"Just take it easy. I'll be right back," Corbett said as he left in search of his friend Sullivan. Sullivan was near the forward bulkhead of the compartment lying on the deck. Corbett knelt next to him, picked up his hand and felt his pulse.

"He's not dead. I can feel a pulse. I think he's hurt pretty bad, but he's still alive." Not wanting to move him, Corbett retrieved a blanket from a nearby locker and covered him. "You're going to be alright, old man. You've just got to be," he said in a tone of desperation.

White came up the ladder from the lower level, "There's four guys down there, two dead. Jiminy is alive but he's hurt real bad. Elvis is banged up pretty good. He's unconscious. We'll have to wait and see." He sat down on the deck next to Corbett and rested his head on his arms across his knees. "What are we gonna do?" he asked in a low voice with somewhat of a whimper.

"Knock it off!" Corbett shouted. "I'll tell you what you're going to do. You're going to get back down there and see if you can help Cricket and Elvis. I'm going back to see if I can locate anyone else."

"I'm not going back down there. You didn't see what I saw. Kelly's lying down there in the bilge. It looks like half his head is gone. It's terrible."

"I don't feel like or have time to argue with you, White. Just get your ass down there. Now move!" White stood up and hesitated before climbing back down the ladder. Corbett headed for the other end of the compartment. There, he found Franklin unconscious in maneuvering. He tried to make him as comfortable as possible. "I hope you're alright, old buddy. If you're not, you're out of luck. I'm no doctor."

White reappeared up the ladder. "I guess Elvis is gonna be alright. He's coming around. I just can't tell about Jiminy. Don't think he's going to make it. I can't do anything else for him."

"Be quiet and listen," Corbett said. "Is that water I hear running?"

"It sounds like it," White replied as he walked toward the other end of the compartment. "It's coming from somewhere in the lower level aft."

The two men hurried to the other aft end of the lower level. The large propulsion shaft, which turns the propeller, had torn loose from the turbine drive gears. Water was pouring into the boat from around the warped shaft packing gland leading through the hull.

"Get the large torque down wrenches!" Corbett ordered. "We've got to get that water stopped and fast."

White returned shortly and the two men went to work tightening down the packing around the propeller shaft. The level of the water in the bilge was rising fast. As the packing gland tighten around the shaft, the flow of the water began to slow.

Wooden wedges driven in with a sledgehammer made the final seal. "That's the best we can do," White sighed as he sat down to rest. "It's just about stopped."

Corbett and White realized that they were very tired. The shock of the incident was now taking its toll on their strength. In their haste to stop the flooding, they had not noticed the body under the forward end of the shaft. A groan came from that direction.

"What was that?" White asked.

Corbett made his way forward along the shaft.

"It's Mister Eddy. Give me a hand. Let's get him out of here."

They inspected the shaft and discovered that it was resting across the lieutenant's left arm just below his elbow.

The impact of the boat had thrown Lieutenant Eddy down the port bulkhead to the lower level. He was attempting to climb back to the upper level when the boat hit the bottom. The shaft tore loose from turbine bull gear and pinned him against the bulkhead.

Corbett and White worked feverishly to free him. They were able to locate two chainfall hoists and attached them to the shaft. The links of the chains strained under the heavy load as they pulled with all their strength. The chain of one of the hoists suddenly snapped throwing them to the deck without budging the shaft.

"It's no use," Corbett said. "We'll never move it with these small chainfalls."

Lieutenant Eddy was semi-conscious. A small stream of water from the pipe above was pouring down his shoulder. He tried to speak but the pain engulfed him, and he fainted.

"I'll get some morphine out of the first aid locker. I guess that's all we can do for him," White said in a somewhat defeated tone.

Later, the two men returned to maneuvering and dropped to the deck totally exhausted. Lee hobbled into the area and joined them.

"How's your leg?" White asked.

"Okay, I guess," Lee replied. "At least it's not broken. I can move it alright. I tried to call the forward compartments on the phone and intercom. There was no answer. I guess all the forward compartments are flooded."

"Do you mean… they're all dead?" White asked. "We're the only…"

"You've got it," Lee replied.

"It looks like Francis is coming around."

Franklin sat up and leaned against the bulkhead.

"How you doin', Francis?" White asked.

"Alright I guess," Franklin replied shaking his head to clear the dizziness. "I've got a hell of a headache, that's for sure."

"You just take it easy for a while," Corbett said.

"I wonder how deep we are?" White asked.

"Check that pressure gage on the bulkhead," Corbett remarked.

White walked over to the gage, illuminated it with a light and slowly counted the markings pointing to each one with his finger.

"This damn thing isn't working right," he said. "It reads 810 psi."

"Let me see," Corbett said with a nervous tone to his voice. He closed the isolation valve and vented the air from the gage. After opening the isolation valve, he stared at the gage for few seconds and then leaned against the bulkhead realizing the obvious. "It's working alright."

"What's the matter?" White asked.

"A sea pressure reading of 810 means that we're at… 1800 feet."

"We're what?"

"1800 feet."

"Damn, damn and triple damn!" Franklin remarked. "Thank you, Electric Boat. They sure built this boat good. We are below crush depth and she is still holding up."

"Now that is scary as shit," Lee replied.

"But if we're… how in the hell are we gonna get outa here?" White asked grabbing Corbett's arm and turning him around with a look of panic in his eyes. "We could make an escape from 200 feet; maybe even 300, but 1800 feet, that's impossible."

"Knock it off," Corbett said sternly as he pushed him away. "We couldn't leave the injured even if we could make an escape. Don't worry they'll get us out of here. A deep diving rescue craft or diving bell can attach to the excess hatch and get us out with no problem."

"How are they going to know where to find us?" White returned. "No one even knows we're down here. We're way out here in the middle..."

"I said knock it off," Corbett shouted. "You're only making matters worse. They know exactly where we are. We'll be out of here in no time. We've got other things to worry about right now."

"Like what?" Lee asked.

"Like maybe staying alive," Corbett replied.

From out of nowhere Robishaw came walking into the propulsion control area. "What the hell happened?" he asked.

"Where did you come from, Robby?" Corbet asked.

"What the hell? I don't know. The last thing I remember I was making a qualification walk through on the IC systems with Elvis," Robishaw replied.

"You okay?" Corbett asked.

"Well, I'm not sure. Not a scratch as far as I can tell," Robishaw replied.

Ellsworth soon followed Robishaw into maneuvering. He had managed to climb the ladder from the lower level.

"How are you doing, Elvis?" Corbett asked.

"Think my arm or shoulder is broken. Don't sure. Hurts like hell," he replied as he sunk to his knees holding his right arm.

"We have a lot of guys not doing so well, Elvis," Corbett remarked with a concerned look. "Just hold on for a while and I'll see what I can do."

"I understand. Don't worry about me," he replied.

"I will worry about you," Corbet returned. "I need you, Elvis. I need for you to be okay. Doesn't seem to be very many qualified men left alive."

Ellsworth managed a half laugh. "Nice to be needed by someone I guess," he said with an unexpected smile.

"What's that noise?" White asked.

"We'll never know what's up forward until we go see. I'm going to take a look," Corbett said as he made his way to the forward end of the compartment.

The auxiliary machinery space also appeared clear as he made his way forward to the reactor compartment. He looked through the small glass viewing port in the watertight door into the shielded tunnel leading through the reactor compartment. As he stepped into the compartment tunnel, water was spraying in all directions. Sea water was pouring through the cable packing glands which penetrated the bulkhead into the forward flooded operations compartment. Several feet of water stood in the tunnel lower level bilge and it was rising slowly.

"White, Robishaw, get up here quick!" Corbett shouted.

"You don't have to yell," White said. "I'm right here."

White's unexpected presence startled Corbett. "Don't you ever do that again. Get the toolbox up here quick. We've got to stop these leaks or we're going to lose this compartment."

White and Robishaw returned in a few moments and they again worked quickly to stop the many leaks.

"My God, there's a hell of a lot of pressure on that bulkhead," White remarked. "Do you think it's gonna hold?"

"Only one person knows that, and he likes to keep things a secret," Corbett replied and then wondered how he could make jokes at such an inopportune time.

"I would have been forward if I hadn't decided to work on my system quals," Robishaw explained. "I guess this was my lucky day."

After stopping as many of the leaks as possible, the men sat down to rest.

"I've had it," White said.

Corbet got to his feet. "We're not finished yet."

"Now what?"

"The storeroom in the auxiliary machinery space lower level has a lot of water from minor leaks. Nothing we can't handle. If we don't get that food out of there, we never will," Corbett replied as he hurried down the hatch to the lower level.

They unloaded the many cases of commissary stores and moved them aft to the engine room.

"Go back in the lower level and see how Cricket's getting along. You'd better take him an extra blanket," Corbett ordered.

"Alright. I hate to think about it but what are we going to do with the bodies down there?"

"I'll give you a hand and we'll put them in the storeroom," Corbett replied.

Later, after closing the door of the storeroom, Corbett and White stood quietly in water up to their knees. White removed his hat and covered his face to hold back his emotions.

"I think you should say a few words," White said. "I guess it's about the closest thing they'll ever have to a burial."

"No, I can't," Corbett lowered his head and replied with some difficulty. "I've never been a religious man. Just doesn't seem right for me to try at this particular moment. He knows what kind of men they were without me telling him."

After checking Sullivan, Corbett returned to maneuvering and fell to the deck exhausted. He suddenly became a little emotional and thought he might cry. His weakness surprised him. He quickly suppressed his emotions. *"It must be fatigue,"* he thought.

White appeared next to Corbett and sat down. He lowered his head to his arm across his raised knees, "Jiminy won't need the extra blanket. He's dead," and wept. "Before he died, he asked for you, Corbett. He also asked me to find his teeth. He didn't want to lose them."

"Get that out your system," Corbett said slowly, "and then get hold of yourself. I think we all need rest. There's nothing else we can do now."

Later Corbett took the time to check Ellsworth's shoulder and arm. His shoulder appeared to be simply out of joint. "White, help me hold him down. Not sure I can do it but I'm going to try and put his shoulder back in place."

"Oh shit!" Ellsworth remarked as he tried to pull away from White's grip.

Corbett held Ellsworth's right shoulder and rotated his arm above his head. As expected, he yelled out in pain and appeared to be almost unconscious.

Corbett made a makeshift sling for his shoulder. "That should do it. At least I hope it will," Corbett remarked.

"Thanks, buddy," Ellsworth replied. "I'm thinking it feels a little better."

"You just take it easy for a while," Corbett continued.

The sailors collected what clothing and blankets they could find and adopted maneuvering as a living space. The area must have been chosen because it was closed in by the three control panels, an electrical panel and the starboard bulkhead. The closeness gave the men a feeling of security as they huddled together on the hard deck. Surprisingly, they had little trouble drifting off to sleep.

The engine room of the sunken hull slowly became very cold, chilled by the water of the ocean depths. Condensation formed on the inside of the bulkheads like beads of sweat and rolled in tiny streams to the bilge. Ocean currents as strong as a stormy breeze passing over the torn metal of the forward superstructure caused it to flap and creak at irregular intervals.

The trapped sailors slept huddled together shaking in the cold damp air. Corbett sat up quickly; suddenly awaken by a loud noise of unknown origin. He looked around and soon remembered where he was. A pain in his arm made him flinch as he ran his hands through his uncombed, thick black hair. He shuttered as the chill traveled up his spine.

As he licked his dry lips he thought, *"wish I could brush my teeth."*

The insignificant idea made him grin. He slid backwards and leaned against the bulkhead. Instinctively, he pulled a cigarette from his pocket and lit it. The taste was repulsive to him and he quickly extinguished it. He sat for a long time thinking and staring at the opposite bulkhead.

His mind would wander back to other times and then suddenly returned. *"Is it a dream? Is it reality? It seems like I've lived this moment before."* A chill ran up the back of his neck. He shuddered. *"I can't remember... can't be happening... it is.... glaring sun... a green field...it's cold...home for Christmas...Mom...Nonie. It's cold."*

He felt very alone and pulled the blanket up to his neck. A drop of water fell from the overhead and splashed in a small puddle on the deck next to him. He blinked his eyes. The few battery powered lights were growing dimmer as they lost their strength. *"It'll be pitch black before long,"* he thought as he looked at the sleeping men around him.

His mind tried to wander again as he fought to concentrate on the inevitable. He had read several articles on deep diving operations at deep depths. An operational deep diving vehicle; capable of executing a rescue at this depth, as far he knew, had not been developed. He didn't want to admit it, even to himself, but doubted if rescue was even possible. The hull also had to be located or the question of rescue was irrelevant. *"We might as well be on the moon as just over the horizon. Best not to express my concerns to anyone,"* he thought. The time had come for a decision on what to do; he made it.

"White, Lee, Francis, wake up! You too, Robby! Elvis! Come on, up and at'em guys."

"What's the matter?" Lee asked.

"Just wake up. We have things to do."

The men reluctantly stirred from their prone positions.

"How do you feel, Elvis?" Corbett asked.

"Pretty good. My shoulder feels better."

"How about you, Francis?"

"I'm okay. I guess I've got a hard head and a glass jaw, and damn it, Corbett. Don't call me Francis."

"Didn't ask but my leg hurts like hell," Lee remarked.

"Don't start slacking on me, Lee," Corbett said with a stern look. "I noticed earlier that you were walking fine."

"Whatever," Lee replied.

"Whatever my ass, I'm going to need your help," Corbett said. "It's obvious that we're the only ones on board left alive."

"It's hard to believe that they're all dead," White said with a sigh.

"You can believe it," Corbett returned. "And it's a very good possibility that we could be joining them soon."

"And what does that mean?" White asked.

"I don't know how long it's going to be before they locate us, or how long it will take to get us out of here after they do."

"I thought you said…"

"I know what I said White and I didn't really know what I was talking about," Corbett interrupted. "Just shut up and let me finish. Our major problem right now is our air supply. I would say that we have enough air to last a week maybe two. We'll know exactly after we got a good inventory of the small oxygen bottles in the compartments and the O2 generator storage bottles in the aft ballast tanks."

"We don't have that long," Lee remarked.

"Why do you say that?" Corbett asked.

"I've been keeping track of the rate of rise of water in the bilge. We're still taking on a lot of water from all the leaks in the piping systems and bulkhead penetrations. The level is rising about an inch an hour. In a week, without pumps, we'll be up to our ass in water. We may be able to slow it down a little but not much."

"Oh shit!" Robishaw said as he pushed himself back and sat against the bulkhead. He covered his head with his arms and his entire body was shaking. He was rocking back and forth muttering, "Oh shit, oh shit."

"What the hell is the matter with you?" Franklin asked. "You in pain or what?"

"Feels like I can't breathe, in a damn box, box is getting…smaller. I need, need …fresh air," Robishaw mumbled as he struggled to answer.

Corbett reached down and pulled Robishaw to his feet by his collar and looked straight in his face. "Straighten the fuck up, Sailor. I need you to suck it up, man up or whatever. You got that?" he shouted as he slapped him several times on his head before throwing him violently back to the deck.

Robishaw just continued to lay on the deck with his hands over his head in a fetal position.

"I want a straight answer from you, Robby. What the hell is going on with you?" Corbett continued in tone of total anger.

"Sorry, just lost it for a minute," he replied. "Felt like everything was closing in me. It happens sometimes but never like this. Couldn't stop it this time."

"You have got to be shitting me," Corbett yelled back. "You have claustrophobia?"

"I guess that's what you call it," he replied.

"Damn shit for brains," Franklin shouted. "You're on a submarine and have claustrophobia. How in the hell have you lasted this long?"

"Just wanted to be on submarines. That's all. I'm fine now," he replied.

"Fine my ass," Corbett interrupted. "How can I depend on you to get it done when it really counts?"

Lee interrupted, "May I remind everyone again that we have a major problem on our hands? Bilge water is going to be over our heads if we don't think of something. I would say that is much more important than this candy ass's state of mind or lack thereof."

"The hull leakage to the bilges just adds more justification to my plan," Corbett returned. "If we're going to survive until they find us, we need power. Our only hope is to bring the reactor critical."

"That's crazy," Franklin remarked. "How in the hell are we gonna do that? The main storage battery forward is flooded. We don't have power to pull the control rods and bring the reactor up to power. Not to mention power for the condenser sea water, feed water and reactor main coolant pumps. You can also throw in the lube oil pumps in for good measure."

"There's a gasoline emergency generator in the lower level," Corbett replied. "We can jury rig it to the reactor rod control power supply. Once the reactor is at power, we can get the steam generators online with convection heat flow from the reactor without the main coolant pumps. Convection flow through the condenser and sea water should also work."

"Will that work?" White asked. "Without cooling pumps, I mean."

"In theory, yes," Corbet replied. "We'll just have to see. We can rotate the other feed water and lube oil pumps we need to limit the load."

"That's impossible," Franklin stated. "Even if we could rig a power supply to the rectifiers for the rods, there are a dozen other things that could stop us. The collision could've jammed the control rods."

"What's the matter with you people?" Corbett shouted. "Are you going to just sit here on your ass until you die?"

His expression was stern as he continued. "Well, let me tell you… I'm not ready to die, not without a fight. I don't know if we can get the reactor up to power or not, but we'll never know until we try. Now knock off the negative attitude and come up with some constructive ideas."

The men sat very quiet.

The silence was broken when White remarked, "Well, let's don't waste any more time and get at it."

"I think I know how I can rig the emergency generator to the DC rectifiers," Franklin remarked. "All I need is 120 volts AC to the power supply box in the tunnel for the control rod drive motors."

"That's great, Francis," Corbett replied. "Good to have another qualified ET and reactor operator that knows the systems."

"Don't call me Francis damn it."

"The carbon monoxide exhaust from the gasoline engine could be a problem," White added. "I think I may just have a way to handle that."

Corbett smiled as he sat down. "Break out some chow, Robby. Let's have some breakfast."

"Right away," Robishaw replied. "What'll it be, tuna fish, sardines or peaches? I think I know where I can find a case of crackers if anyone wants some."

"I like sardines with crackers," White remarked.

Lee threw a blanket over White's head. "You can have them all."

"Get the peaches but hold the crackers," Corbett said with a laugh.

"I'll have a steak medium rare with eggs over easy," Franklin remarked with a smile.

Robishaw tossed him a can of peaches. "Sorry, your chef is off duty."

"I'll pass on the food right now," Ellsworth remarked. "Don't have much of an appetite."

Corbett threw him a can of peaches. "Try and eat something. You need your strength and I will need it too."

Ellsworth said nothing as he accepted the food and then asked for a second.

The men were in good spirits as they ate hungrily. They also ate quietly, each with their own thoughts, fears and doubts; but all with the same hope. They knew they were alive and that was the important thing. After eating they must tackle the problems at hand.

"Robby, I want you to conduct an inventory of all the support equipment and oxygen cylinders," Corbett said as he pulled Robishaw up from the deck. "Can you get that done?"

"Will do."

"Elvis, your job will be to look after Chief Sullivan and Mister Eddy. Think you can handle that with your bum shoulder?" Corbett asked.

"Can do," he replied.

"Shouldn't we try again to get Mister Eddy out?" White asked. "We can't just leave him there."

"That shaft and the bull gear weigh over twenty tons," Corbett replied. "It would take a crane to lift it. We've done all we can. If he's lucky, he won't live much longer."

"That's a terrible thing to say," White returned.

"I'm trying to be realistic," Corbett said as he rested his head on his forearm against the bulkhead. "Lee, you can break out the UQC emergency underwater telephone. Transmit our call sign every five minutes. It plugs into the hydrophone connection there on the bulkhead."

"I have a question," Lee explained. "Should we be transmitting our call sign over the UQC in the clear? I would think that is classified."

"I admire your concern for the integrity of classified information, Lee, but I could really give a shit at this point. Just get the UQC," Corbett interrupted.

"Who gave you the authority to tell us what to do? I don't think..."

"I don't give a damn what you think, Lee!" Corbett shouted as he turned around quickly. "Now let's get something straight here and now. With Chief Sullivan and Mister Eddy hurt, I'm the senior petty officer. As far as you're concerned, I'm the commanding officer of this boat. Any questions, anyone?"

White shook his head no while the others only stared at the deck.

"Get at it then. Elvis, give Mister Eddy another shot of morphine if the pain gets very bad. Take it easy. There are only a few syringes left in the first aid locker. Francis, you can help if he needs it."

"Aye, aye, Captain," Franklin replied. "And my name is Franklin."

"Don't be a wise ass," Corbett returned. "Just do what you're told."

"I'll do what you say, Corbett, but just don't push it," Franklin added.

"I'm going to check the reactor and the steam plant," Corbett said and walked away as if he didn't hear the remark.

Lee inspected the UQC emergency underwater telephone, flipped the many switches and plugged it into the hydrophone connector. He spoke slowly and clearly into the microphone. "Any station, this is *(Redacted)*, Any station, this is *(Redacted)*, over." The sound echoed and vibrated back over the speaker as it traveled through the water. No answer was expected or received. White stood, lowered his head and walked away. Franklin and Robishaw followed.

The sailors set about in their effort to survive. They realized that their world would be limited to the confines of the sunken hull for what could be a long time; a world which was only 270 feet long and 20 feet wide. It was a hostile world which was slowly becoming smaller and would not support life. The first essential elements, food and fresh water, were in abundance. The supply storage locker had contained ample food to feed a dozen men for many months on a diet of canned peaches, tuna fish, sardines, flour, sugar and coffee, but no coffee pot. The freshwater tanks were full and intact. The most important element, air, was quickly being depleted and presented an immediate danger as well as the rising sea water in the bilges.

Robishaw completed the inventory and stood talking with Franklin and White in the reactor compartment tunnel. Corbett entered through the watertight door from the auxiliary machinery space, dressed in white overalls, rubber gloves, rubber boots, a white cap and a face mask.

"Dr. Ben Casey, I presume?" White said with a laugh.

"Very funny," Corbett said. "Quit wasting time and start work on the connections for the emergency generator. I'm going to check the reactor compartment."

"I guess you know," Franklin remarked. "If there's any broken piping down there, the airborne radiation could spread everywhere and kill us all."

"What difference does it make if you're drowned, suffocated or radiated; the end result is the same. You're dead. Do you have any better ideas? If not, knock off the chatter and get that gasoline engine up here," Corbett said as he opened the access hatch and dropped quickly into the reactor compartment.

"That guy had better get off my back," Franklin remarked.

"Why don't you tell him that?" White asked.

"Maybe I will."

"Take it easy. He's not such a bad guy. If you knew him as well as I do, you'd realize he's just putting on an act," White replied.

"Well, he'd better not push me again."

The reactor compartment was very white and clean. The reactor in its simplicity appeared rather sinister as it sat in the center of the compartment. Corbett inspected the reactor vessel and discovered that a large portion of the boron radiation shielding around the reactor had broken off. It was obviously damaged from the impact when the boat hit the submerged mountain and the ocean floor. He climbed back to the tunnel and closed the hatch. After changing clothes, discarding any possible contamination, he sat down on the deck to rest. Franklin, White and Robishaw were waiting for him as him after he emerged from the reactor compartment.

"We have a problem," he said. "The shielding around the reactor is partially damaged."

"And that means what?" Robishaw asked.

"It means that if we get the reactor up to power, the background radiation level in the compartment and here in the tunnel will probably be excessive," Corbet replied. "Not sure how much of a problem that will be yet. Hopefully we can just limit the time we spend in the tunnel to keep our radiation dose to a minimum. Won't be able to enter the reactor compartment when the reactor is critical and at equilibrium that's for sure."

"Dose...dose of what...critical...what does that mean...like a problem...what?" Robishaw continued.

"Oh crap! Knock it off with the reactor theory questions, Robby," Franklin interrupted. "Just do what we tell you to do and don't do anything else. You'll be fine. Doubt if we'll be able to get the damn thing up to power anyway."

"You're right, Francis. We need to get back to work," Corbet remarked as he headed back toward the engine room.

"Damn it!" Franklin shouted. "I've told all of you that I don't like to be called Francis. Frank is okay. Franklin is okay but not fuck'n Francis."

"Right, Francis, now get busy with that portable generator," Corbet ordered as he disappeared through the watertight door.

He stopped on his way aft and knelt next to Sullivan. With a shell-shocked look, he grabbed Sullivan's wrist and felt his pulse. He slowly folded the Chief's hands across his chest and pulled the blanket over his head. Sullivan was dead. *"Why him? How is the decision made; who's to live; who's to die; when and where?"* He walked slowly into maneuvering and stood with his head lowered on his crossed arms against a panel. He suddenly stepped back and hit the panel with his fist. The pain was welcome.

"What's the matter?" Lee asked.

"Sullivan's dead."

"He's better off."

Corbett grabbed Lee by the collar and pulled him up from the deck. He drew back his fist but suddenly stopped.

"Just like you, I was only being realistic," Lee said with a frown.

He pushed Lee backwards to the deck and walked quickly away.

Franklin and White carried the small gasoline engine to the reactor compartment tunnel and set it on the deck. The reactor compartment tunnel ran through the compartment containing the nuclear reactor. The tunnel allowed personnel to travel through the compartment protected from the high-level radiation illuminating from the nuclear reactor inside.

"I guess we ought to test it before I go to all the trouble of wiring it to the panel," Franklin remarked.

"Why, have you got something better to do for the next couple of days?" White asked.

"You're beginning to sound just like him."

"Who?"

"You know who. Corbett."

Corbett stuck his head through the watertight door from the auxiliary machinery space and asked, "How are you doing?"

"Okay! We were just going to test it," Franklin replied.

"Forget it. Just wire it up," Corbett added as he turned and disappeared.

Franklin only smiled at White and walked forward in search of the materials he needed. Corbett continued his inspection of the steam plant and found that the plant was operational utilizing the cross-connect and components from both the port and starboard sides. Later that day, the men ate their second meal and rested.

"I wonder if it's day or night," White remarked as he lay on a blanket.

"What difference does it make?" Lee asked.

"I'd just like to know what I ate, breakfast, lunch or supper."

"You two had better get some rest," Corbett remarked. "We still have a lot to do and not much time to do it in."

He looked at Lee again and noticed something. "What's that in your belt?" he asked.

"What does it look like? It's a 45 pistol," Lee said.

Corbett sat up quickly. "Give it to me."

"What?"

"You heard me. I said give it to me."

Lee hesitated, pulled the gun from his belt, looked at it and handed it to Corbett.

"Where did you get this?" Corbett asked as he examined the gun and two clips of ammunition.

"It's a standard piece of equipment in the abandon ship kit," Lee replied.

Corbett shoved in a clip, put the extra clip in his pocket and placed the gun in his belt. "Wouldn't want you to get hurt," he said.

"Hey that's mine. I found it. You've got no right to do that."

"Get some sleep," Corbett replied as he lay back down and covered his head.

Lee mumbled something and turned over to sleep.

The hours passed slowly; Corbett slept only a short time. He lay in his makeshift bed staring at the overhead. He thought once of waking the others and getting back to work; but decided to let them sleep. Sometime later, he gave up the idea of sleeping, gathered some shaving gear together and climbed down the ladder to the lower level. After drawing a bucket of water, he lathered his face and started to shave. His only blade was dull and pulled his thick beard. The cold water only added to his problem. Afterwards, he washed himself, changed into a clean set of work overalls, washed the dirty clothes and hung them to dry. As he worked, his thoughts were varied. He caught himself, thinking of a particular dark-haired girl with a nice ass in a tight leather skirt. He quickly shook off the thought and climbed up the ladder.

"All right you guys, it's time to get at it," he said.

The men stirred under the blankets and managed to sit up.

"Damn, Corbett, where are you going, on a date?" Lee asked. "Aren't you pretty?"

"You could stand a shave, yourself," Corbett returned. "And take a bath. You stink to high heaven."

"No, thanks," Lee remarked. "I'm just fine."

"I said get yourself squared away. That goes for the rest of you. You're sailors, not a bunch of pigs. You'll shave, bathe, and change clothes every day."

"You're a riot," Franklin remarked. "Here we are, not knowing if we're going to live another week and you're worrying about how we look."

"I don't give a damn how you look. In fact, I don't think a shave would help you very much."

Franklin gritted his teeth and started to stand up when White grabbed his shoulder and pulled him back.

Corbett continued. "I do care how you feel. If you're clean, you'll feel better and optimistic. You'll work harder. Now, get at it!"

The men ate another meal of peaches, all but White. He ate four cans of sardines. After eating they continued their assigned tasks.

Later that day, preparations were completed, and they were ready to attempt a reactor startup.

White filled the small engine with gasoline. He grabbed the starting lanyard, hesitated and then pulled with all his strength. The other men watched in anxious anticipation. The engine turned over but failed to start. On the second try, the engine hesitated, started and picked up speed quickly. The engine exhausted through a hose leading to the sealed reactor compartment.

"Isolate the panels for the forwarded compartments, Franklin, and close the breaker," Corbett ordered. "I'm going to the maneuvering room. You come with me, Robby. I might need your help."

By the time Corbett and Robishaw reached the reactor control panel, the instrumentation and controls were energized and operating normally. He sat down in his chair and quickly put the control rod switch to the raised position. The bottom indicators on 10 of the 12 control rods dimmed and then went off as the rods started their upward travel. The small engine slowed and stalled dropping the rods back into the reactor.

"You're overloading it," White yelled from the tunnel.

"I know it," Corbett replied. "I'll pull half of them at a time. Two of the rods are stuck, but I can still bring it up to power. Get that engine started again!"

The engine started, and the reactor control rods started their upward travel once more.

The nuclear instruments electronically measured the minute particles which traveled within the reactor. Like the cycle of human reproduction, neutrons struck and fertilized the uranium atoms. In a sudden burst of life, many new neutrons and heat were released to live a life measured in thousandths of a second, one generation giving birth to another, the next larger than the last. As more of the neutron absorbing rods was removed, the cycle became self-sustaining.

The temperature and pressure in the reactor raised slowly and, likewise, the pressure in the steam generator.

"I have a delta temperature in and out of the reactor," Corbett yelled. "There's convection flow between the steam generator and the reactor. I think it's working. Damn! Am I smart or not?"

Corbett shouted, "Francis, we've got 50 psi of steam. Start bringing the plant online."

"Right," Franklin yelled as he opened the many steam valves leading to the auxiliary turbine.

Since he qualified in submarines, Franklin is very knowledgeable in the operation of the engine room steam and turbine systems even though his specialty was electronics. Before he earns his Dolphins (Submarine Service insignia), each man aboard is expected to accomplish the jobs of others in the event of just such an emergency.

"Francis, you can put a steam generator feed pump online!" Corbett yelled. "When you are ready to roll the steam turbine, light off the lube oil pump."

"You'd better hurry up," White shouted. "There's not much gas left. If you don't get that ship's service generator on the line pretty quick, you can wrap it up and call the movers."

"I'm going as fast as I can," Franklin replied as he started the turbine lube oil pump and steam generator feed water pump.

The steam turbine slowly picked up speed as Corbet opened the throttle. The frequency of the generated electrical current increased as the speed increased.

Franklin shouted from the lower level, "I have adequate feed water in the condenser and a delta temperature with the sea water. Must also have convection flow in the condenser sea water system. You were right again, Corbett."

"That's all the speed I can get until we get more pressure in the steam generators. We need the main cooling pumps on the line.

Your convection heat flow theory from the reactor isn't working very well, Corbett," Franklin shouted,

"That'll have to do," Corbett replied from his position in the maneuvering room.

Franklin climbed the ladder from the lower level and entered maneuvering. "What's going to happen when you put that big turbine generator on the line in parallel with that small engine?" he asked.

"One of them is going to trip open," Corbett replied.

"Which one?"

"I don't know. Could be both."

"Won't the control rods drop when the power shifts?" Franklin asked again.

"If I knew the answer to that, I wouldn't be so nervous," Corbett replied.

When the frequency of the turbine generator matched the output of the small emergency generator, Corbett grabbed the turbine generator power breaker switch and closed it without hesitation. The two men stared and gasped as the reactor instruments dropped to zero indicating loss of power and, then, slowly returned to their original positions.

"The engine just stopped, and the breaker tripped," White shouted from the tunnel.

"It's okay," Corbett returned with a sigh of relief. "We're on reactor power now."

"Look, Corbett; reactor temperature is dropping fast."

"Damn it!" Corbett shouted. "Two control rods dropped on the power shift fluctuation."

"Do you want me to shut the steam stop valves?" Franklin asked as he started forward.

"Hell no," Corbett answered. "Maybe I can get the rods back up before I lose too much heat." He was quickly throwing switches in that effort.

"You try that, and you'll drive the reactor prompt critical. You could blow the thing sky high and kill us all," Franklin said sternly.

"We have no choice. Now get up there and cut down on some of the electrical loads so we can keep that generator on the line. Kill the lube pump."

"That'll wipe the bearings," Franklin replied.

Corbett turned around quickly and hit him with a left to the stomach followed by a right to the jaw which knocked him back down the passageway and to the deck. He quickly turned and continued to pull the control rods in his race against the decreasing reactor temperature.

"Kill the lube oil pump, White," he shouted.

"Right away," White answered.

The temperature of the reactor slowly stopped its descent and started upward. At the same time the reactor power level increased at a dangerous rate. Corbett reached quickly across the panel and bypassed the high reactor power safety shutdown just before the power meter pegged. He closed his eyes as he held the bypass switch tightly and waited for a possible explosion. It never came. The power level oscillated for a few moments and became stable at a low level.

Corbett flipped the bypass switch back to normal, slumped in his chair and lowered his head to the panel.

White walked into maneuvering. "Looks like we might just make it," he said. "Somebody up there likes us. The lube oil pump is back on again but I'm afraid the bearings on the turbine are heating up."

"To hell with it," Corbett remarked. "Let it run until it falls apart. If you think it is necessary, shift to the Number Two turbine."

"Do you think you damaged the reactor?" White asked.

"I don't know. It seems to be responding okay. I don't think so."

"Rickover would have a stroke if you knew what you were doing with his reactor," White remarked with a smile.

"Screw Rickover," Corbett replied.

"Who's Rickover?" Robishaw asked.

While holding back a grin White replied to Robishaw, "Don't worry about it, nub. It's not on your qualification card."

"Two control rods are stuck on the bottom," White remarked. "Is that a problem, Corbet?"

"Nope. The reactor is critical and self-sustaining. Just means the reactor fuel will only last maybe eight years instead of ten. Don't think we have to be concerned about that," Corbett replied with a big smile.

"Right, right, I see what you mean," White continued with a louder than normal laugh.

Franklin appeared beside Corbett. "I'm sorry I lost my head. You did it damn it. I didn't think you could do it, but you did it. That power level sure looks good."

"Forget it," Corbett replied. "Line up and get the emergency bilge pump started White. Have one main coolant pumps started and it seems to be working okay. After we get the water out the auxiliary machinery space, you'll have to wash the salt water out the oxygen generator and CO_2 scrubber equipment. Let it dry and get it on the line. We are not out of the woods yet."

"Aye, aye, Capt'n," White replied as he all but skipped down the passageway.

"Do you think the emergency bilge pump will discharge to sea against this high sea pressure?" Franklin asked.

"Like I said before. We'll never know until we try. That's what is was designed to do so we will see," Corbet replied and it was obvious that he was annoyed by the constant pessimistic questioning by Franklin.

"Bilge pump started, discharging to sea and the water level in the lower level seems to be going down," White reported.

Corbet only looked at Francis and smiled.

The men began to feel better as the steam system removed the chill from the air and normal bright lighting was restored.

Franklin stared at the reactor panel. "Corbett, I think you're increasing the temperature in the reactor too fast and the pressure is too low. You need to let the pressure increase or you'll start boiling in the reactor."

"Would you just shut the hell up, Francis," Corbett replied. "I know what I'm doing. I'm just on the edge of the safety range. This is the quickest way to get to operating temperature and pressure and still minimizing the risk of excessive reactor vessel stress. Just dig out the manual if you think I'm wrong."

"Well, I don't think you'll get to 480 degrees and 2000 psi the way you're going now without some serious damage."

"Our target parameters are lower since we are not operating the main propulsion turbines. We only need reactor temperature and steam generator pressure for the auxiliary power turbines. Just in case you may have forgotten Francis, this boat is not going anywhere," Corbett replied with a smirk.

Franklin hesitated and thought for a moment before leaving maneuvering without another word.

The sailors worked throughout the night drying and cleaning the large electrical motor and components of the oxygen generator. The air was becoming very stale. All the surplus oxygen bottles had been bled down and were empty. During the reactor start up the small gasoline engine had used more of their oxygen than anticipated. In the thin air, the men could only work a short time before they had to rest gasping for air. It was a race against time.

Corbett sat at the reactor panel watching the many instrument meters and maintaining the reactor at a steady power level and temperature. Franklin appeared beside him.

"How's it going?" Corbett asked.

"Not too good," Franklin replied. "The emergency C02 discharge compressor motor is still indicating a short circuit. We've cleaned and dried every inch of the motor with no luck.

There must be some salt residue from the sea water in there somewhere. We just can't get to it."

"How are the other components?"

"No problem," Franklin replied. "The heaters are operating satisfactory. I had to replace a couple of shorted switches. They've been tested and are operating satisfactory. We're all ready to go except for the compressor drive motor."

"Have you tried washing it with fresh water?"

"Yeah, but still no luck," Franklin replied. "I just don't think we're going to be able to clear it."

"We may have to try and run it anyway."

"I guess you know if you start that motor now it could burn out the windings? Not sure if the CO_2 compressor is even going to discharge against the pressure at this depth anyway so then there is that," Franklin said.

"Like I said before, we have no choice. If it doesn't work, it doesn't work. We'll face that problem like all the others when we get to it."

"Just as you say," Franklin returned. "Give the word and I'll give it a whirl."

Corbett thought a few moments. "Do it."

"You're the boss," Franklin said as he turned and walked away.

Lee was stationed at the power switch in the upper level of the auxiliary machinery space. Franklin and White watched the motor in the lower level.

"Light it off," Franklin shouted.

"Power on," Lee replied as he flipped the switch.

The large motor began to turn and made a whining noise as it picked up speed. Suddenly a large arc flashed in the viewing window of the motor. Sparks and bits of burning metal spewed across the deck.

"Shut it off," Franklin shouted.

"Don't have to," Lee replied. "The power breaker tripped on overload."

"I guess that just about tears it," White said as he attempted to look through the viewing window of the smoldering motor. "This thing'll never run again."

"We'd better give the bad news to Corbett," Franklin said.

"Just one thing," White said.

"What's that?" Franklin returned.

"Don't say that you told him so. It was his decision to make and he made it."

"That decision could just be the end us and you're still going to stick by him?" Franklin remarked.

"Yes, I am," White replied. "If it wasn't for him, we wouldn't even have had a chance."

"He made the decision. He's in charge and he's responsible," Franklin replied.

"I think you'd be willing to die just to prove him wrong," White said. "Are you really that jealous of him?"

Franklin didn't answer but only turned and climbed the ladder to the upper level. The men had gathered in maneuvering. An atmosphere of defeat prevailed. The disappointment of their failure was evident in the faces as they communicated in silence.

"So close and yet so far," Franklin remarked as he removed his torn shirt and threw it to the deck.

"All we need is a spare motor," White said.

"That's it," Corbett said with a smile slapping White on the shoulder.

"That's what?" White asked.

"A spare motor," Corbett replied. "We need a spare motor."

"Yeah, but we don't have one," Franklin added in a tone of curiosity.

"We've got a whole engine room full of motors," Corbett said. "The Number 2 feed water pump motor is about the right size and we don't need it."

"It doesn't run at the same speed," White said as his smile turned to a frown. "We could never find a motor that runs anywhere near the same speed."

"That's no problem," Corbett said. "We could add a different size pulley and connect to the compressor shaft. A pulley twice as large would run at half the speed as its prime mover."

"It just might work," Lee said as he sat up.

"You damn right it will," Corbett said. "We're going to need the welding rig so bring it out of the lower level."

"That's going to take a long time," White said taking a deep breath. "I don't know if we have much time left. This air is getting pretty thin."

Franklin slapped Corbett on the back. "I guess we'd better get started then, right boss?" he said with a smile.

"Right," Corbett replied. "Lee, you take the watch on the reactor. I'm going forward."

"Will do," Lee replied.

"What can I do?" Robishaw asked.

"Stay with Lee on the reactor panel. He can show you what to do," Corbett replied.

"Reactor panel?" he asked with hesitation. "I've never done that. That is not on my qual card. I was told that I would not have to learn the reactor. I'm not an engineering nuke."

"I won't tell anyone, Robby," Corbett returned. "It's not that hard to learn. All you have to do is keep TAV in the reactor at 350 degrees by raising the control rods up and increasing the power level a little. If you drive TAV too high, just push the rods back in a little. It doesn't take much rod movement to bring the power level and TAV back to normal. This low range power level meter here should be here at zero when you are not moving rods. That indicates the reactor is critical and stable with no change. The reactor pressure stays at about 1,000 psi and steam generator pressure of at least 400 psi. It's just that simple."

"What's TAV?" Robishaw asked with a concerned look as he sat down at the reactor control panel. "You haven't told me yet what critical means. You also haven't said anything about these TH and TC meters. What should I do with them?"

Corbett shook his head, mumbled something under his breath and walked away.

"Okay, Robby. Forget everything he told you," Lee interrupted. "Just do what I tell you and don't do anything I didn't tell you."

"I didn't know that you are qualified, Lee," Robishaw remarked. "When did that happen?"

"Never you mind," Lee replied. "Corbett and Francis say that I am reactor qualified and that's all you need to know."

"Will you tell me what critical means?" Robishaw ask.

"Why in the crap don't you just shut the fuck up and do what you are told, Robby? That's it," Lee replied with a somewhat puzzled look. Obviously, Lee could not explain.

The men removed the feed pump from its mounting in the lower level of the engine room and pulled it to the upper level. It took all the strength they could muster to drag it forward to the auxiliary machinery space and lower it down the hatch. After removing the burned-out motor, they slid the new one in place and collapsed on the deck drenched in sweat.

"Now it's in place," Corbett said as he lay on the deck grasping for breath. "Put on the fly wheel, White. I'll bolt it in place while you put on the pulley and attach it the CO_2 compressor, Francis."

The exhausted sailors rested for a few more minutes before continuing their task. The jury-rigged compressor motor was soon ready for testing.

"Turn it on," Corbett shouted from the lower level.

"Switch on," White replied. The motor started and quickly picked up speed. Franklin began to close the many switches on the control panel.

"Bleed some oxygen into the compartment, White before you send it the storage tanks," Corbet ordered with a sign of relieve. "The CO2 should start to clear out soon."

"Aye, aye, Skipper," White returned with a wide smile.

"CO2 is discharging to sea but only at half capacity," Franklin reported.

"That's okay. We don't have CO2 from 100 people to worry about," Corbet remarked sarcastically.

Cool fresh air slowly began to flow through the air ducts leading aft from the fan room. White stood under an outlet vent, removed his white hat and let the air blow over his head. The men expressed their joy in laughter and cheers. Their joy would not last long. Survival was now not something to be obtained but enjoyed. It would soon become something to be endured.

SitRep 5-To be Endured

The days that followed were uneventful. The men rotated the watch on the steam plant and the reactor control panel. When not on watch, they read what few books were available and sat around telling sea stories. Most of the time, they slept. Occasionally, the question of rescue would be discussed and always end in an argument. On the eighth day of their imprisonment, an incident occurred which would have a permanent effect on the men.

"Throw me a can of tuna," Franklin said as he sat at the reactor control panel.

"Catch!" White complied and threw the can right on target.

They were gathered in maneuvering area eating.

"I hope I never see another peach again," Lee remarked.

"Try some sardines," White added.

"You and your stinking sardines," Lee continued. "If you leave those smelly cans lying around again, I'm going to shove them up your ass."

"Knock it off," Corbett interrupted. "Just consider yourself lucky that you have anything to eat."

"It's about time for you to relieve me, Corbett. I'm beat," Franklin remarked.

"Okay, I want to finish this," Corbett said as he wrote on a pad of paper.

"What are you doing?" Lee asked.

"I'm writing a letter."

"You're what?" Lee returned with a laugh. "How are you going to mail it? Give it to the next porpoise that passes by."

Corbett didn't answer.

"Who are you writing to?" White asked.

"His girl I bet and isn't that sweet," Lee remarked. "True to the childhood sweetheart to the end, or is it to a particular sexy, tall brunette that we all know and love in our home port?"

Corbett looked up and stared at him.

"Do you mean Corbett has a local girlfriend?" White asked. "How come you never told me about her?"

"Yeah, Corbett, why haven't you told him about your girlfriend?" Lee asked with a smirk.

"Just shut your mouth, Lee," Corbett said. "Don't pay any attention to him. He's just running off at the mouth."

The conversation was interrupted by a loud moan from the lower level.

"It's Mister Eddy," Corbett said. "I guess I'd better take a look."

He hurried down the ladder and made his way aft along the shaft to the lieutenant's location.

Lieutenant Eddy was semi-conscious. The dripping water from the overhead had dried on the side of his face leaving salt flakes clinging to his shaggy beard. He had developed infection in his crushed arm and had a high fever. He opened his eyes and looked at Corbett as he forced some water down his throat and washed his hot face with a damp cloth. "How long has it been?" the lieutenant asked.

"About seven maybe eight days…I think."

"I'm sorry I can't accommodate you and die. God knows I've tried."

"You're going to be alright, Sir. Don't you worry."

"Don't soft soap me, Corbett. I've had it. This is…." He was unable to complete the sentence as the pain became worse.

"Help me," he said. The pain was evident in his twisted face.

"I can't," Corbett said quickly as he lowered his head. "The morphine is all gone."

"Then, kill me," the lieutenant returned as he grabbed Corbett's arm and squeezed it with surprising strength.

Corbett searched for something to say but could only remain silent.

"If you can't do it, leave me that gun."

Corbett pulled his arm away, turned and hurried away. He entered maneuvering, fell to his bed and stared at the overhead.

"What's the matter?" Franklin asked.

"Mister Eddy is out of his head. He wants…" Corbett hesitated. "He wants the gun to kill himself."

"Why didn't you give it to him," Lee remarked. "He's going to die anyway."

"I can't stand to think of him in pain," Franklin said.

"I'm sure you're concerned about him," Corbett returned. "I haven't seen you taking care of him."

"That remark wasn't necessary," Franklin said.

Lee added, "As far as I'm concerned, I can't stand to hear him scream anymore. He's driving me crazy."

"I think we should put it to a vote," Franklin said.

"Vote on what?" White asked.

"What were we talking about, you moron. We vote to see if he should die," Franklin returned.

"That's crazy," White said as he stood up.

"That's a good idea," Lee added. "I think Mister Eddy's vote should..."

"That's enough," Corbett interrupted. There'll be no voting. I'm in charge, I'm responsible and I'll make the decisions. Give me your knife, Lee."

"My what?"

"I said give me your knife."

"What are you going to do?" White asked.

"I'm going to get him out of there."

"The only way..." he paused, "you can't do that," White said.

"It's the only way," Corbett returned. "Get the gas bottles and boil a lot of water. I'll need as many clean rags as you can find. Give him a hand, Lee."

"I guess you know that it will kill him if you try to cut it off," Lee remarked with a smirk.

"That's terrible," Franklin added. "You'll kill him."

Corbett shook his head. "You guys really get me. First you said you wanted him dead and now you're afraid I'll kill him. Just give me the knife and do what you're told."

The men hurriedly made the preparations. White picked the knife from the boiling water and handed it to Corbett. As Corbett turned to go below, White spoke. "I don't know why you're doing this, Corbett. It's insane."

Corbett stopped, turned and listened to White. "Maybe you think you're helping him. You can rationalize it away if you want, but the end result will be the same. He will be dead. You know what you have to do so just do it for God's sake." Corbett turned without saying a word and went below.

He crawled down the shaft next to the lieutenant and sat looking at him. Lieutenant Eddy opened his eyes and returned the look. Corbett stared at the shaft resting across his arm just below the elbow.

"I'm sorry, Mister Eddy. I don't know what else to do." Corbett said with watery eyes. "If the situation were reversed, maybe you could handle it better."

The lieutenant turned his head in the opposite direction without a word. Corbett cut away as much of the soiled clothing as possible. He accidentally touched the arm and the lieutenant flinched in pain.

Corbett sat back, lowered his head and thought for many minutes. Without warning, he quickly pulled the gun from his belt, pointed it at the lieutenant's head and pulled the trigger.

The shot rang out and echoed throughout the compartment. The men topside waiting in anxious anticipation, jumped at the noise of the unexpected shot. They looked at one another but said nothing.

A full hour passed before Corbett suddenly appeared in the maneuvering area and collapsed on his bed. He rolled over on his back and stared at the overhead.

"I thought…"

"I know what you thought," Corbett interrupted. "I don't want to talk about it. Francis, you and Elvis get Mister Eddy out of there and to the storeroom."

"What the…" Ellsworth attempted to say something before being interrupted.

"Just shut your damn trap and get it done," Corbet said as he turned his face to the bulkhead and wept in silence and secrecy.

SubSunk-39 days

The actual date was unknown by the stranded crew of *(Redacted)* when Lee hurried into maneuvering from the steam turbine end of the engine room and said, "We have a major problem!"

Corbett jumped to his feet. "What's happening?" he asked.

"We have a substantial increase in the radiation reading in the upper level of the engine room near the steam turbines. We have a much higher radiation reading in the lower level next to the steam condensers."

"What kind of radiation level are you talking about?" Corbett asked.

"Approximately 20 mrems per hour in the upper level and 100 mrems in the lower level," Lee answered.

"That's a problem but we don't have to panic," Corbet remarked. "Anyone going to the lower level let me know and limit your stay to 10 minutes or less. We can rotate people going below to keep the exposure to 10 minutes maximum if that becomes necessary."

"Alright," Robishaw stated with an unexpected stern look. "It's time for that reactor theory lesson. I want to know exactly what the hell is happening and don't tell me to shut the fuck up."

"I can only give you my best guess," Corbet replied. "Francis you can tell me if you agree. Looks like we may have a buildup of radioactive fission products in the primary coolant from a damaged fuel element. The two control rods stuck in the bottom of the reactor must be damaged which also damaged the adjacent fuel assemblies releasing radioactive products. The fuel elements have a barrier or cladding designed to these keep radioactive products inside the core. This barrier on the fuel assemblies near the two damaged control has obviously been breached."

"How is the contaminated primary reactor coolant getting into the secondary side steam turbines and the engine room?" Ellsworth asked. "I don't know much but I do know that is not supposed to happen."

"We must have a leaking tube in the steam generator that separates the primary and secondary system," Franklin interrupted. "That is the secondary barrier. As a matter of routine there could be some steam generator tube leakage. Never detectable since the possibility of a major fuel assembly rupture is very remote. Again, it's routine to have a small amount of corrosion on the fuel assemblies which causes a small amount of radioactive products in the primary cooling water. Hopefully we are not faced with a severe rupture of the fuel assembly cladding."

"Okay…nice to know information. Can it be fixed?" Robishaw asked.

"Sure, it can be fixed," Lee answered. "All we need do is to pull into the shipyard, shutdown, cool down the reactor, isolate and open up the steam generator and plug a few leaking tubes. I also don't know much but I know steam generators."

"Nothing we can do at this point," Corbett remarked. "We'll just monitor the radiation levels and do what we can to limit our exposure. If the leaking fuel assemblies get any worse, then we don't have to worry about anyone finding us. We'll all be dead. Simple."

"You're right about that, Boss," Franklin remarked as he dropped to his blanket bed on the deck. "I'm going to get some shut eye."

White lowered his head and began to sob.

"Take it easy, buddy," Corbett said putting his arm around his shoulder. "We'll be out of here in no time."

"I wouldn't mind it if it were only me," White said regaining his composure. "It's my wife and kid. I don't know how she'll get along without me."

"Do you really think that slut is waiting for you?" Lee asked in a sarcastic tone.

"Shut your mouth, Lee," Corbett said sternly.

"What do you mean?" White asked as he approached Lee slowly.

"You tell him, Corbett."

"I said shut your mouth, Lee or I'll shut it for you."

"Let him talk," White shouted. "He's got a big mouth. I want to hear what he has to say."

"Ask your friend," Lee replied.

"What is he talking about, Corbett?"

"Don't listen to him," Corbett replied. "He's out of his head."

"You should know who your real friends are," Lee said with a smirk. "Your so-called friend made a run on your dear wife. One of my buddies saw you in the Silver Nugget that night, Corbett, so don't try and deny it. How was she in bed, pretty good?"

"You are a lying son-of-a-bitch," White shouted at Lee as he jumped on top of him.

The men wrestled across the compartment and neither one able to strike a blow. Corbett was about to make a move to separate them when he saw the wrench in Lee's hand. Lee pulled back with the wrench and struck White on the head. White let out a groan and slowly rolled off the top of him.

Corbett kneeled over his friend to examine his wound. Luckily the blow glanced off the side of his head.

Lee scrambled to his feet. "It wasn't my fault," he said anxiously. "He started it. He jumped me. It was a fair fight."

"If he dies, you're going to pay for this, Lee," Corbett said as he worked over his unconscious friend.

Lee stood back with a frightened look in his eyes. Suddenly, he reached down and grabbed the gun from Corbett's belt. Waving the gun between Franklin and Corbett, he backed against the bulkhead. "Don't come near me. I said it wasn't my fault."

"Put that gun down," Franklin said as he stood up from his chair at the reactor control panel.

"Shut up," Lee shouted. "I'm in charge now. You'll do what I say from now on."

"Stay back, Francis. I'll handle this," Corbett ordered. "Come on now. Give me the gun, Lee. You don't want to shoot anyone."

Corbett leaped at Lee and grabbed the wrist holding the gun. He slammed Lee's arm across his leg and the gun fell to the deck. A single blow sent Lee tumbling down the passageway.

Robishaw had already retrieved the gun. "Lee, this is crazy. You are in enough trouble," he shouted.

Lee staggered to his feet. "Like I said, it was not my fault."

Corbett turned and slowly walked back to the location of his wounded friend.

White was conscious as Corbett worked to stop the bleeding from the side of his head. "What happened?" White asked. "The pain is…"

"Don't try to talk, buddy," Corbett said. "You're going to be alright. It doesn't seem to be that bad."

"What he said…it wasn't true was it?" White asked grabbing Corbett's shirt collar.

"You know it isn't true. I did ask her for a date, but I didn't know she was your wife. She turned me down flat and told me where to get off."

"White smiled and let go of his collar. "I knew it. I just had to hear it from you."

"Just don't you go and die on me, buddy," Corbett said jokingly. I need you"

"I'll try not to," White said with a faint smile.

"Lee, you get the hell over and help White," Corbett ordered sternly. "You did this, so you handle it. If we ever get out of here, you'll probably have to answer to a court martial."

"Like I said, not my fault," Lee replied.

"Yeah," Franklin returned sharply. "But you don't bring a damn wrench to a fist fight you stupid ass non-qual nub."

"All right you guys. Knock it off. It's over. I'll stand Lee's watch on the turbines in the engine room," Corbett said as he walked away.

Ellsworth was quiet during the entire episode. "You guys are going absolutely batshit," he said. "Why don't you two just go ahead and kill each other…kill us all. Get it over with. You act as if we don't have enough trying to kill us."

Everyone just stared in Ellsworth's direction but did not say a word. All was quiet. All was calm.

Over the coming days life was aboard *(Redacted)* was becoming more difficult for the small crew of men to handle. Boredom and uncertainty were a constant burden on their minds. Long hours keeping the engineering equipment working properly was a constant burden on their bodies as the days and weeks turned into months. The boredom was, however, to be short lived.

Part Three: Search and Rescue
South of Azores
Location 32°64.9′North 33°18.89′West

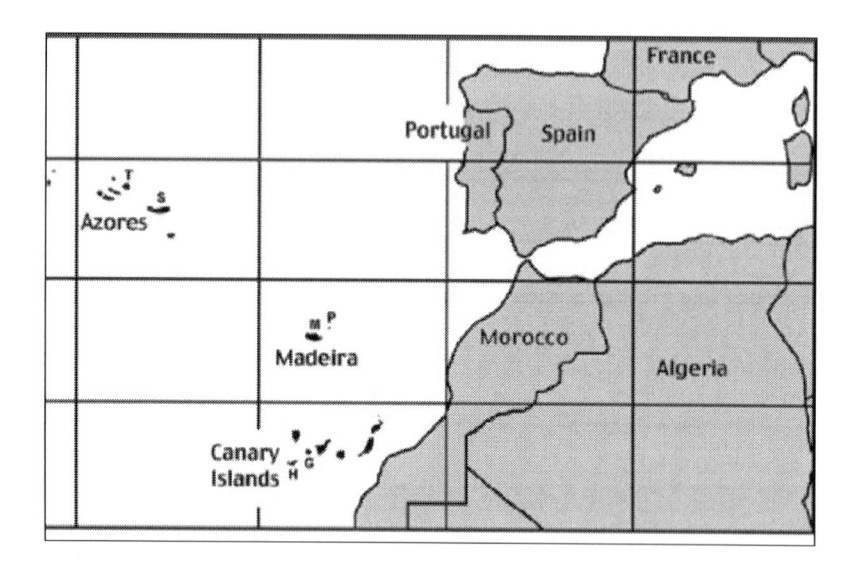

SitRep 6-SUBMISS/Search

SubSunk- 58 Days

The date was 12 March 1968. The commander walked quickly down the long corridor. He dodged with ease the men in uniform entering and leaving the various offices along the way. He carried a briefcase and was careful not to strike anyone in his path. His pace never slowed as he disappeared through a door at the end of the corridor. A sign above the door read:

Deputy Commander Submarine Force Atlantic

He waved to the secretary at the desk and proceeded directly to the inner office.

"Go right in, Commander Hill. The Admiral is expecting you," the secretary said.

Her comment was unnecessary for he had already knocked and entered. Inside, the office was decorated completely in green and looked very distinguished with dark mahogany furniture.

Admiral Harvey Bentley, Deputy Commander Submarine Force Atlantic, is a 25-year veteran of the Navy. He served aboard two fleet type submarines in the Pacific during WWII and made a total of six war patrols. Following the war, he was assigned to the Bureau of Ships and was an assistant project manager for the construction of the USS *Nautilus* and later served as her executive officer. He was executive officer on the maiden voyage of the USS *Skipjack* and later assumed command. He commanded the Fleet Ballistic Missile Submarine *USS George Washington* Blue Crew and one other FBM submarines before his assignment as Commander Submarine Squadron Four in Charleston, South Carolina. He considered retirement but was offered and accepted the job as Deputy Commander Submarine Force Atlantic. He recently divorced from his wife of 20 years. Since he was recently passed over for the job as ComSubLant, he is again considering submitting his request for retirement.

"Good morning, Art," the admiral said as he rose from his chair to shake the commander's hand. "Have a seat."

"Thank you, Admiral," he replied and sat down in the large chair in front of the desk. He could smell a strong order of alcohol from the admiral's breath. "I came as soon as I received your call. Could you brief me further on the details?"

"I am sure you are aware that we have not received a movement report message from one of the submarines in your squadron, the USS *(Redacted)*," the admiral said. "You should have already been briefed on her mission."

"Yes, Sir, I have."

"We should have received a movement report no later than yesterday. The mission was expected to be completed at that time. We've sent a message on every frequency directing *(Redacted)* to break radio silence and report in the clear if necessary. We have not received a reply."

"They could be having communication problems, Admiral."

"I certainly hope that is the case," the admiral said as he picked up a paper from his desk. "I recently received this intelligence report from the Joint Chiefs of Staff. It seems that a Soviet destroyer was sunk about nine weeks ago. The details are sketchy; but, from what I can gather, it was in *(Redacted)'s* patrol area."

"Do you think there's any connection?"

"I didn't think so until another incident occurred during the investigation into the death of one of my staff officers killed in an automobile accident." The admiral swung in his chair slowly from side to side as he continued. "It appears that he was delivering a top-secret message to me at the time of his death."

"Can you divulge any of the information in the message?" the commander asked with a note of curiosity.

That's part of the problem. The only copy of the message was destroyed." The admiral paused, lit his pipe and blew the smoke high in the air. "I have evidence from the radioman who received the message that it was transmitted by *(Redacted)*."

"Do you think the message concerned the Soviet destroyer?"

"It must have," the admiral replied. "It's my theory that the destroyer attacked the *(Redacted)* and she returned the fire. Indications are the destroyer was torpedoed. *(Redacted)* must have also been sunk in the engagement but was first able to get the message transmitted. Long range passive sonar also picked up explosions which could have been depth charges."

"I guess that's possible," the commander remarked, "but…"

"But what?" the admiral asked. "Do you have any other ideas? If you do, speak up. That's why I asked you here."

The commander rose from his chair and walked to a large map of the Atlantic hanging on the wall. "I was just going to say, Admiral, if I were the commanding officer of that submarine and if my boat was damaged to the extent that it was in danger of sinking, I wouldn't take the time to code a distress message. I would send it in the clear."

The admiral leaned back in his chair, folded his arms and puffed on his pipe. "What's your theory, Art?"

"Well, Sir, I'm trying to put myself in Commander Flynn's position. He has just engaged and sunk a destroyer. If I were him, I'd send out an incident report and high tail it for home sending out a movement report as soon as possible." He turned and approached the admiral as he continued. "Something happened shortly after the incident report was sent which prevented him from sending the movement report."

The admiral nodded indicating approval. "The question is where is she now?"

Commander Hill turned and stared at the map for a few moments. "She could be having communications problems, or it could be something much worse. In any case, Captain Flynn would be proceeding to port at best possible speed. I would first assume that *(Redacted)* cleared the Straits of Gibraltar. Search along this line and you should find the *(Redacted)*," the commander added with a quick sweeping motion across the map. "If necessary, ComSixthFleet could then assume the search area east into the Mediterranean. Phase Three would involve routine NATO aircraft searches further east to the Black Sea. At that point I would not expect her to ever be located. I would assume she is lost and position unknown."

The admiral hesitated and said, "As I recall, we do have intelligence reports of two single screw nuclear submarines transiting through the Straits of Gibraltar about eight weeks ago. They were picked up on our ocean bottom sonar arrays between the Canary Islands and the Azores. Because of the ocean conditions at the time, we lost contact. They were not identified and assumed to be Soviet submarines going back north to the Baltic."

"Even more reason to assume that the first place to search should be west of Gibraltar," the commander remarked. "Any evidence of any conflict between the two submarines? (**Redacted**) could have been sunk during an encounter with a Soviet submarine."

"No traffic concerning such an encounter has been intercepted," the admiral replied as he returned to his desk. "Any torpedo explosions in the area would have been picked up by our ocean bottom sonar arrays."

The admiral leaned forward, folded his arms on his desk and looked down as he thought for a few moments. He removed the pipe from his mouth and knocked the ashes into an ashtray on his desk. He mumbled something as he dusted an ash off his neatly pressed, white uniform. Flipping the switch on the intercom on his desk, he called, "Larry, set up a staff conference in thirty minutes to discuss SUBMISS alert and preliminary search procedures for (**Redacted**)."

"Right away, Admiral," the voice replied over the intercom.

The admiral rose from his chair and walked over to the commander. Shaking his hand again, he said, "I want to thank you for your comments, Art. A fresh new approach from one of the best officers who ever commanded a submarine is always helpful."

"Thank you for the compliment, Admiral, but in my opinion, you were the best. I still have your footprints on my backside. I was not one of your most promising junior officers."

"That's true. You weren't," the admiral replied with a laugh as he walked him toward the door and then stopped. "I want you to coordinate the search, Art. You can set up shop in the Communications Center."

"Just as you say, Admiral. When are you going to notify the next of kin of the crew?"

"I will make my recommendation for publication of a SUBSUNK message ninety-six hours after the preliminary air search and notify the next of kin at that time," the admiral replied. "There's still a good possibility that we could find the *(Redacted)* adrift and disabled somewhere. I personally believe she's lost."

"That seems like the most logical explanation for her silence," the commander said.

"We'll find her, no matter how long it takes. If we don't, we'll never know what happened," the admiral said as he continued toward the door. "Good luck, Art, and keep me informed of any developments so I can pass them on up the line. Needless to say, this is important. The Chief of Naval Operations, himself, has been on the carpet for this one and he wants some answers."

"I understand, Admiral," the commander replied as he opened the door to depart.

"I also assume that you been fully briefed on *(Redacted)'s* classified experimental RPJ propulsion system?" the admiral asked.

"Yes, Admiral. I have. I have been briefed on its progress from installation and testing as well as its success during sea trails. I am anxious to find how it performed during spec ops," the commander replied.

"It's imperative that *(Redacted)* and her propulsion system not fall into Soviet hands. If the Soviets were able to get a passive sonar pattern for *(Redacted),* you can bet your sweet ass that they were trying to track her," the admiral said sternly.

"I understand completely, Admiral," the commander replied as he departed.

Commander Arthur Hill, recently selected for captain, is a man of average height with exceptionally dark hair. He looks very young for his age. At forty he was the youngest man ever to be assigned as a Squadron Commander. He commands a squadron of eight submarines with an iron hand and will not hesitate to relieve any commanding officer who does not perform to his standard.

Commander Hill quickly formulated the search plan for the *(Redacted)* and established communications with responsible Commands. Long range anti-submarine warfare aircraft under ComAswForLant were dispatched in a search pattern along the suspected track of the missing submarine. All submarine squadrons and rescue vessels were placed on standby alert to get underway on one-hour notice. The search for USS *(Redacted) (SSN-Hull Number Classified Secret)* had begun. SubMiss notice was released that evening on 12 March 1968.

The clouds were large and formed odd white shapes in front of a background of blue sky. The green, glossy surface of the ocean below stretched from horizon to horizon in all directions. In the distance, a dark object appeared from the clouds and grew larger as it approached. It soon took its true shape of an aircraft flying low over the surface of the water. The pilot and co-pilot were searching the surface from their side windows.

"No luck, Bill and it's about that time," the co-pilot said anxiously to his pilot.

"Yeah, I guess you're right," the pilot answered as he picked up the microphone to his radio. "Home Plate, this is Tango Charlie Two, over."

A voice answered over the speaker. "Tango Charlie Two, this is Home Plate, send your traffic, over."

"This is Tango Charlie Two. On station time completed… running low on fuel… returning to Home Plate. No joy on search pattern, over."

"This is Home Plate, I roger your traffic. Interrogative your course, angels and position, over?"

"This is Tango Charlie Two. My course zero-niner-five, angels 300. My position north Area Alfa Three, climbing to angels 10,000 for the return trip, over."

"This is Home Plate, roger. I'll see you at the club tonight, Bill. I'll buy the first drink."

"This is Tango Charlie Two. I just might take you up on that, Chuck. I'll see… Wait one, Home Plate! I have an object in the water. I'm going back to take another look. I'll contact you later, out."

The pilot replaced his microphone, pulled back on the throttle and banked the aircraft to the left as he turned to retrace his track.

The aircraft traveled very fast a mere hundred feet above the water on its next pass. The co-pilot pointed out the window at an object on the water. It was bright orange and contrasted sharply with the light green water. After several passes over the object the pilot called, "Home Plate, this is Tango Charlie Two. I have an object in the water at my previously reported position. It appears to be an orange life jacket adrift. I'm pretty sure that it's the type carried on submarines."

"This is Home Plate, roger. You'd better head for home, Bill, before you're too low on fuel."

"If I leave now, Chuck, they may never be able to locate that life jacket again. Someone has to stick with it. Another aircraft will be in my area in about an hour. It's a long-range boat plane and can land to pick it up. I can hang around until then."

"Don't take a chance, Bill. Drop a flare and get the hell out of there now. I'll vector you."

The communication was interrupted as the pilot flipped off the switch on the radio. He gave his co-pilot a thumbs up. The co-pilot smiled and shook his head in agreement.

The air traffic controller called the aircraft repeatedly with no answer. He checked his equipment but found nothing abnormal.

After what seemed like an eternity, a voice came over the traffic controller's speaker. "Home Plate, this is Tango Charlie Two, over."

"Bill, where in the hell have you been?" the controller asked as he grabbed the microphone.

"Don't get excited, Chuck. We just had a minor problem with the radio. The boat plane just landed to pick up the life jacket and I'm at angels 10,000 on the way home."

"How's your fuel?" the controller asked in a concerned tone.

"Don't worry, Chuck. We'll make it. This is Tango Charlie Two, out."

The Communications Center was a flurry of activity. Commander Hill stood next to a large overlay of the Eastern Atlantic and Mediterranean Sea on a long table. Several men were positioning model ships and planes at various locations on the map.

Another officer approached the commander and handed him a message. "Why don't you try and get some sleep, Commander?" the lieutenant asked. "I can take over here for a while. You've been on your feet for over thirty-six hours."

"I'm okay. If we haven't found anything in another six hours, I'm calling off phase one of the search. Write up search instructions for a pattern a hundred miles to the west."

"Will do, Sir."

A radioman hurried over to the commander and gave him a message. "Sir, we just received this report from Air Wing Twenty-Two out of Rota, Spain. An aircraft picked up a life jacket in area Alfa Three. It has definitely been identified as coming from (*Redacted*)."

The commander marked the area on the map. "There's no telling how far it's drifted, but at least we have a clue now."

"I would say that she's definitely down in that area somewhere," the lieutenant said. "If we localize the search, we'll probably find more debris."

"Locating her is still going to be a problem," the commander said as he studied the map. "The minimum depth in that general area is 3500 feet. The pressure at that depth would crush the hull like a pancake."

"No, Sir, that's not exactly true," the radioman beside him said.

"What do you mean, Sailor?" the commander asked. "Do you know something about the pressure of sea water that I don't?"

"No, Sir, I was referring to that specified depth. The depth in that area is not 3500 feet. The contour lines on that map are not up to date. There's a plateau here in this general vicinity with a depth of 300 fathoms," he said making a circling motion with his hand on the map, "and a mountain peak about here with a shallow depth of 500 feet."

"Where did you get this information?" the commander asked.

"We received a Notice to Mariners about nine or ten weeks ago. The area was recently surveyed by an oceanographic vessel which supplied the information to the Coast Guard. I put the message out on the broadcast to all ships myself. I remember it because it came in the night the communications duty officer was killed."

"What was the priority?" the commander asked.

"It was broadcast as a routine message since there were no submarines transiting that area and went out the following day."

The commander studied the map for a few moments. "Get me a copy of that Notice to Mariners right away," he said as he took his slide rule and made a few quick calculations. "Also get me an updated map. This damn thing is useless."

The radioman returned shortly with Notice to Mariners number 214.

"Get the deputy commander on the phone right away," the commander ordered as he studied the message.

"Aye, aye, Sir," the radioman replied.

The commander sat down at his desk and made notes on a pad as he spoke to the lieutenant. "Write up a SUBSUNK message for release. Dispatch all ships to Alfa Three. I want a complete bottom contour of that area."

"Do you think she hit that submerged mountain?" the lieutenant asked.

"The parts of the puzzle are fitting together," the commander said shaking his head in acknowledgement. (*Redacted*) must have had a communications problem just after sending the incident report. They never received the Notice to Mariners and were unaware of the submerged mountain range. I would say they went down about eight to nine weeks ago."

"All that ocean and they had to cross that particular spot," the lieutenant remarked shaking his head. "The chances of hitting that mountain would be a million to one."

"The chances just happened to go against them, I guess," the commander said. "I'll inform the admiral of our theory. As soon as he gives the okay, I'll release the SUBSUNK message. Get New London, Connecticut on the line in the meantime. Issue orders to Warrant Officer Banyan to embark on the USS *Sunbird* out of Norfolk. The Sunbird will get underway as soon as Banyan is on board."

"Right away, Sir," the lieutenant said as he departed.

The general area where (*Redacted*) went down had been located through the efforts of a brave pilot, a conscientious radioman and a dedicated commander. The submarine search aircraft, Tango Charlie Two, was later listed as missing and never heard from again.

The search beneath the sea had only just begun.

SitRep 7-SUBSUNK/Rescue

SubSunk-61 Days

The date is 15 March 1968. The bright morning sun shined through the window of the small apartment. Articles of clothing were scattered about the floor; dirty dishes were stacked in the small sink; empty beer bottles covered the small kitchen table. A single chair, couch and small bed completed the items in the sparsely furnished room. A man was sleeping in the bed. His short bright red hair on his head matched the hair on his freckled arms. His snoring vibrated throughout the room. His name is Warrant Officer Victor Banyan.

Banyan is an experienced diver and the Navy's leading expert on deep depth salvage operations with 18 years of service. For four of those years, he served in the Coast Guard. He conducted most of the initial tests in the development of deep diving rescue vessels. His hobbies in private life are limited to drinking and women. He has been married three times none of which lasted very long. His job is his first love and occupies most of his time. His assignments usually take him to all parts of the world for long periods of time on a moment's notice.

His deep slumber was suddenly interrupted by the telephone ringing next to the bed. He fumbled for the receiver, picked it up and laid it next to his ear on the pillow. "Banyan here."

"Yes Sir, but I'm on leave now," he said to the voice at the end of the line.

He sat up in bed suddenly and rubbed the sleep from his eyes. "Yes, Sir. I'll be on the next plane," he said and replaced the receiver as he slid from the bed.

In thirty-minutes he had shaved, showered and dressed. For the first time he noticed the female still asleep in his bed. She was bare from the waist up covered only by a sheet. He looked closer. She was obviously a somewhat older lady, probably in her early sixties but could have been a little younger and, in his opinion after a second look, not very attractive at all.

He lowered his head, looked away and appeared rather confused as he ran his hand through his red hair trying to remember the night before. "*Oh yes*," he thought with a sheepish grin and then a quiet laugh. "*Oh yes indeed. Oh well, any port in a storm so they say but this appears to have been a damn Cat 5 hurricane.*"

He quickly finished the remnants of a bottle of beer on the table and hurried out the door to an awaiting taxi which would take him to the local Naval Air Station. Four hours later, he reported aboard the submarine rescue vessel USS *Sunbird* (ASR-15) in Norfolk, Virginia. The *Sunbird* had just arrived in Norfolk after being dispatched from operations north near Narragansett Bay.

The duty officer escorted Banyan to the Commanding Officer, Lieutenant Commander Kenneth Edwards.

"Come in, Vic," the captain said as he rose from his desk. "It's good to have you aboard. We'll be getting underway shortly."

"Thank you, Captain. It's good to be serving with you again," Banyan said shaking his hand.

"We rendezvous with the destroyer *Madison*, at 1400 tomorrow and transit north east. We'll be in the search area just south of the Azores in about ten days. I assume you've been briefed on our mission."

"Not exactly," Banyan replied. "All I know is what I've read in the SUBMISS alert."

"(*Redacted*) is believed to be down in this area here," the captain said referring to a chart spread over a table. "Two sonar equipped ships are converging on this position. After we complete a bottom contour sweep, we should have the hull just about pinpointed. We will also be assisted by the submarine USS *Pargo* (SSN-650). The two-man deep diving vessel, Telstar IV is being airlifted from the west coast and will be transported to the area. It should be on station by the time we're ready for the descent to take photographs."

"I'm acquainted with the Telstar IV. Who's my co-pilot?"

"Warrant Officer Page, my diving officer," the captain replied.

"I know John. He's a good man. What's the water depth in the area?"

"1800 feet on the plateau and about 3500 feet further west."

"How long ago did she go down?"

"About eight to nine weeks ago is the best estimate at this point."

"No chance of survivors after this much time," Banyan said. "Just as well, I guess. Rescue from that depth would be a problem. I would say that at that depth she is a crushed hulk of metal on the bottom."

"Our job is to locate the hull and photograph it. If salvage isn't possible, we're to use Telstar to destroy any portion of the hull left intact to prevent future salvaging by foreign nations. Write up your operational plan and submit it to me for approval."

"Aye, aye, Captain. I'll have it ready," Banyan said as he studied the chart. "It's going to be rough. It's a muddy bottom and the current is pretty strong. The Telstar only has a submerged capability of several hours. We'll be lucky if we even sight it in that bottom terrain."

"We'll find it no matter how long it takes. Make yourself at home. You look like you're pretty tired. Get some rest and I'll see you after we get underway. As I said, we should be in the search area in about 10 days but could be a little sooner."

"I could use some rest. I had a hard night last night."

"You'll never change, Vic," the captain said with a laugh. "How do you work all day and play all night?"

"As I recall, you were a pretty hard charger in your younger days."

"Just a minute now. I'm not that old. I've just settled down a little."

"You're getting soft and a middle-aged bulge," Banyan said as he patted him on the stomach.

"Just good home cooking."

"We'll have to swap some sea stories later," Banyan remarked as he turned to leave the stateroom.

"Yeah," the captain replied. "Just like old times."

"See you later, Ken," Banyan said as he departed and made his way to his own stateroom.

The rescue vessel *Sunbird* got underway for the rendezvous point. She was 250 feet long and carried a crew of about 120 men. Built in 1950, her primary mission was shallow water salvage. Installed salvage equipment included a diving bell capable of rescuing personnel from a sunken submarine down to a maximum of 350 feet. The four bright orange pontoons carried on the side were used to raise small sunken ships from a maximum depth of 200 feet. She was as useless as a rowboat in deeper water but was the best the Navy had to offer.

The following morning, the *Sunbird* was cutting its way through the high waves of the Atlantic Ocean on its way on a northwest great circle course. An occasional spray of water over the bow covered the forward deck of the small ship with foam which would quickly drain over the side. The sky was gray and completely overcast.

Banyan appeared on deck from a hatch amidships and walked forward along the railway of the ship. He was bundled in a foul weather jacket and a small pull-over cap. Steam formed in the cold breeze from the hot coffee in the cup which he carried in his hand. He braced himself against the railing momentarily as the ship took a sudden roll to starboard. He stood near the bow and allowed the cold spray to pepper his face. He took a deep breath and shuddered in the cold morning air. The coffee was hot and burned his lips as he attempted to take a drink.

"You're going to catch a cold," a voice said behind him.

Turning around Banyan saw his old friend John Page. "Hi, you old sea-horse. Good to see you again," Banyan said with a smile shaking his hand.

"Good to see you too. I thought you were going to sleep forever."

"Yeah, I was beat. That's what I like about going to sea; I can always sleep good. I'm always a little sea-sick the first day out I guess."

Banyan's friend towered a full foot above him with very light blonde hair and a thin build.

"I'm glad we'll be working together," Page said. "I've got a funny feeling about this one, Vic."

"What do you mean?" Banyan asked. "We've had tougher assignments than this one."

"I know," Page returned. "I guess I'm just getting old and soft."

"Remember the dive we made in the St. Andes Trench off California? That one was 15,000 feet. This one will be like a dip in the pool."

"I know, but I'm still glad you're here," Page said.

"Have you had any experience in a Telstar IV vehicle?"

"No, not much. Just Telstar I."

"It's a simple little machine and not much difference from the first version. We'll make a few practice dives before the deep one," Banyan said as they turned to go inside. "Come on. I'll buy you some breakfast."

The two men disappeared through the hatch amidships.

SubSunk-70 days

Unknown to the men onboard *(Redacted),* the date was 23 March 1968. Without a sunrise or sunset, working clock or calendar, they had long since lost track of the days. One day soon merged with the next and become one long endless hour by hour and then, dreadfully, minute by minute. For the past several weeks, the men had made very little effort to keep their minds occupied. They ate, slept and waited. Religion had been discussed several times but not one man had knelt in prayer. Their attitudes could only be explained by the uncertainty of their situation. Survival was now something to be endured. How long they didn't know.

"Any station, this is *(Redacted)*. Any station, this is *(Redacted),* over." There was no answer. Lee turned off the underwater telephone and replaced the microphone. He shifted his position while sitting on the hard deck and stretched his arms high above his head. He fought to stay awake. As he looked around, he saw his three shipmates. White was sitting at the reactor control panel while Franklin and Corbett were sleeping. Lee closed his eyes and listened to the whirling sound of the turbine and support machinery. In a few moments, he drifted off to sleep.

"Hey, Lee, wake up!" White shouted. "You're supposed to be on watch. It's time for a transmission."

"Yeah, okay," Lee replied. "A lot of good it's going to do. I've talked into this thing until I'm hoarse."

"They'll find us," White said. "It won't be long now. I just know it."

"Yeah, sure." Lee said. "Wake up Franklin and Corbett. It's time for them to relieve us."

White shook the two sleeping men. They stirred reluctantly. Corbett sat up and rubbed the sleep from his eyes. His hair was a tangled mess. The growth of beard on his face indicated that he had not shaved in many days. His clothes were surprisingly wrinkled and dirty.

"How about relieving me, Francis?" White asked.

"What's your hurry?" Franklin asked. "You going somewhere?"

"No, it's your turn on watch. You always stall around, and I end up taking half your turn."

"I'll take the watch when you give me back my book," Franklin returned.

"I haven't finished it yet."

"You've had it for a week. You must have read it twice by now. It's the only book I have. I want it back."

"Why don't you two knock it off?" Corbett interrupted. "You sound like a couple of kids. He'll give the book back when he's finished with it."

"You're always taking his side," Franklin said as he stood up. "It's mine and I want it."

"Give it to him," Corbett said. "I can't stand his belly aching."

"Okay," White said. "I didn't know he was going to get so hot under the collar. It's just a little old book. I don't even know if I know where it's at now."

"Well crap, you'd better find it, you stupid hillbilly," Franklin shouted.

"When we get out of here, I'll buy you another one," White replied.

Franklin grabbed White by the shirt collar and pulled him to his feet. "You're always rattling your mouth off about being rescued. It's always tomorrow, just wait till tomorrow. You might as well get use to the idea that you're never going to get out of here. You're going to rot here just like the rest of us."

"Take your hands off him," Corbett said as he stood up, "or maybe you'd like to try that on me."

Franklin shoved White back against the bulkhead and sat down at the control panel without a word.

Lee remained seated on the deck eating peaches from a can with a knife. "Damn! How about that," he remarked. "The captain has finally shown some emotion. You haven't talked that much in a week."

"Mind your own business," Corbett replied. "What I do is not your concern."

"I wish I had a big strong man to take care of me," Lee continued. "I could use a bodyguard with a big gun who likes to shoot people in the head."

Corbett turned around quickly, injected a shell into the chamber of the gun and placed it against Lee's forehead. Lee froze with his mouth open and a peach dangling in mid-air on the knife. They only stared at one another without a word for many moments.

"You say one more word and I'll show you just how much I like it. Come on big mouth say something," Corbett said sternly.

"Hey you two," White said. "This is going too far. Just take it easy."

Corbett let the gun slowly fall to his side as he turned away. Lee placed the knife in the can and sat it down next to him. "You're a big man with a gun in your hand," Lee remarked.

"I can take you with one hand tied behind me," Corbett replied as he lay down on his blanket and covered his eyes with his arm.

"I didn't mean to cause trouble," White said. "I have to believe that we're going to get out of here. It's the only thing that keeps me going. I don't think I could stand it if I thought I wasn't going to see the wife and kids again. I bet she's worried sick. She has always been so dependent on me."

"Sure, I bet she has," Lee said with a grin.

"What do you mean by that remark? Don't start that shit with me again, Lee!" White yelled.

"Knock it off," Corbett interrupted as he suddenly sat up. "Can't you hear it?"

"Hear what?" White replied.

"I can't hear anything," Franklin said.

"Be quiet and listen," Corbett repeated sternly.

The men listened. A noise slowly became audible and grew louder and louder. The dull pinging sound in the distance echoed within the sunken hull.

"It's sonar!" Franklin said.

"They're here," White shouted. "They've found us. I knew they would."

The sailors expressed their joy by dancing around in a circle, cheering and laughing.

Corbett rushed to the underwater telephone. "Any station, this is *(Redacted)*. Any station this is *(Redacted)*, over." He repeated the call many times but received no answer.

They listened for a long time as the sonar grew louder, but then slowly began to fade. Soon, all was quiet again.

White slowly dropped to his knees and lowered his head. "Why didn't they answer? Why didn't they stop?"

"Don't worry," Corbett said. "They'll be back. They couldn't have been over a few thousand yards away. We could hear them, but they couldn't hear us with the active sonar pinging."

"They're not coming back," White said. "They have no reason to search this area again. We're going to die here." He sobbed softly.

"Shut up you sniffling baby," Franklin said. "I'm tired of listening to you."

"Knock it off!" Corbett shouted. "I hear sonar again."

"I can hear it too," Lee added. "They're coming back."

"Just relax," Corbett interrupted. "The active sonar pinging is still covering up our transmission. We'll have to wait until they switch to passive. Hopefully the active sonar has at least picked up an echo from the hull."

The sonar pinging became loader and louder before trailing off into the distance.

On board *Sunbird* Warrant Officer Page entered the officer's wardroom and sat next to his longtime friend Banyan. Page is a widower with two girls in high school. As an enlisted sailor, Page was a chief boatswain's mate before obtaining the rank of warrant officer. On board surface ships boatswains' mates train, direct, and supervise personnel in ship's maintenance duties in all activities relating to deck, boat seamanship, painting, upkeep of ship's external structure, rigging, deck equipment, and boats. In addition, they also serve as boat coxswains. Like Banyan, Page is also a qualified deep-sea diver and salvage expert. His most notable assignment was the investigation into the sinking of the USS *Thresher* (SSN-593) lost with all hands during deep diving tests, 10 April 1963; 129 died. He photographed the wreckage of *Thresher* during a deep dive aboard Telstar I in early 1964.

"The weather seems to be picking up to the east," Page remarked. "Could be getting some thunderstorms, rain and high winds today and tomorrow. Maybe we should hold up on the Telstar dive for a few days."

"Might be the wise thing to do. Let's wait for the morning weather reports," Banyan continued. "I understand the ETA of Telstar has been delayed so the weather may not be an issue. We can take a look at the bottom contour maps the sonar escort vessels have developed. They reported the 500-foot mountain range and 1,800-foot plateau have been located. The contour maps should give some indication of a hull if it is there on the shallow plateau."

"Yes," Page replied. "If the sub landed on the bottom off the plateau, it would be at a depth over 3,000 feet. That is going to make it much more difficult to locate. Have you thought about a demolition plan if salvage turns out not to be an option?"

"Not as yet," Banyan replied. "We have a demolition team aboard one of the escort vessels. We'll get their input as soon as we locate and inspect the hull."

"Think I'll go topside to the bridge," Banyan remarked. "I want to review the latest contour maps."

"Okay, Vic," Page replied. "I'll be up shortly."

Banyan climbed the ladder leading to the bridge and asked to enter the bridge area. "Permission to come aboard," he asked the officer of the deck.

"Permission granted," the young officer on watch replied as he gazed around the horizon with his binoculars. He was assisted by two lookouts on watch who also manned binoculars. Another sailor stood at the ship's helm maintaining the ship on the course.

Banyan stood listening to the pinging sonar coming over the speaker. He listened more intensely. He thought he heard something strange and very faint coming over the speaker.

He turned to the officer of the deck. "OD would you request that the escort vessels stop active sonar and go passive?"

"Well do," the officer replied.

The sonar pinging suddenly stopped.

On board *(Redacted)* Corbett picked up the underwater telephone turned the volume on full and called continuously. The other sailors looked on nervously. A faint broken transmission was received over the UQC underwater telephone speaker.

"Station calling…again…calling…say…over." The transmission became weaker and weaker as it traveled deeper through the ocean.

Corbett spoke very slowly and distinctly. "Any station, this is *(Redacted)*, over."

"*(Redacted),* this is *Sunbird*. I hear you loud and clear. How me, over?"

A roar of cheers erupted from the sailors.

"We're as good as out of here. Talk to him, man," White said.

"This is *(Redacted)*. I hear you the same. My name is Petty Officer Corbett. There are five other men down here. Their names are Don Ellsworth, Don White, Ted Franklin, Michael Lee and Robert Robishaw, over."

"This is Warrant Officer Banyan on board the rescue vessel *Sunbird*. Is this some kind of joke or am I really talking to the crew of the *(Redacted)*?"

"This is no joke. We're the only ones left alive. Can you get us out?"

"I don't know how you guys have managed to survive this long, but just hold on. We'll get you out as soon as possible. I want you to give a continuous long count so we can get your approximate location. I'll get back to you later, out."

Corbett gave the microphone to Lee and he commenced a continuous count transmission. The sailors were in good spirits as they settled down to await their rescue. They tried to relax but were too excited. The excitement would later again turn to doubt as the wait turned into hours, days and then weeks.

SubSunk-71 Days

The date is 25 March 1968. At ComSubLant, the conference room is very large. At one end, a chalkboard and map were positioned for easy viewing. A large oval table sat in the center. Pads of paper and pencils were neatly placed at each chair. Some of the chairs were occupied by various high-ranking naval officers. The remaining chairs were quickly filled by officers still entering the room. A steward in a white jacket passed among the officers pouring coffee. Some talked with their neighbors alongside or across the table, while others sat in silence.

Commander Hill entered and stood at the head of the table next to the chalkboard. When everyone was seated, he spoke. "If I could have your attention, Gentlemen, we'll begin. Some of you have already been briefed on some of the details of the situation. I hope this conference will clarify any misconceptions and answer any questions which you might have."

"The USS *(Redacted) (*Hull Number-*Redacted Classified Secret)* is sunk resting on the bottom in 300 fathoms of water in area Alfa Three located about here just northeast of the Canary Islands," the commander said as he pointed to the map at 32°64.9′N 33°18.89′W. "The bow compartment and operations compartment are flooded. The engineering compartment including the engine room, auxiliary machinery space and reactor compartment are intact. There are six survivors trapped in the sunken hull."

"When did she go down?" one officer asked.

"About 8 to 10 weeks ago. That is the best information we have at this time," the commander replied.

"How in heaven's name have they survived this long in such a confined area?"

"By some miracle, they were able to bring the reactor up to power. The oxygen generator and carbon dioxide burners are operating normal. They have an ample supply of food and water and are in no immediate danger."

"That's fantastic" another officer remarked. "We must recommend these men for a commendation."

"Before we start passing out medals, we have to get them out," the commander replied. "Presently our rescue capability is limited to 350 feet. DSRV deep diving rescue vessels are under development, but not one is currently operational. I'm sorry to say, Gentlemen, but the situation looks very grim."

The deputy commander stood up slowly from his chair, "I have orders to get those men out no matter what. Funds are unlimited. How much do we need to complete the development of a rescue vehicle?"

"I'm afraid it's not a question of funds now, Admiral. It's a question of time. It would take at least two years to complete such a task. I'm afraid you're too late with your offer. You should have been more generous with the DSRV program funding sooner."

"That remark was unnecessary, Art. You know that I receive guidelines on the expenditure of funds just as you do."

"I apologize, Sir. The remark should not have been directed at you personally, Admiral."

"Are you saying the situation is hopeless?" the admiral asked.

"No, it's not hopeless. There's a chance; a slim chance, but we have no alternative. We must use what equipment we have available. A new type of rescue ship the USS *Pigeon* (ASR-21) is presently under construction at the Alabama Drydock and Shipbuilding in Mobile. Its large, double hull catamaran allows for more accurate moving over a sunken hull. It was originally designed to carry a deep diving rescue vehicle. It presently has a diving bell aboard designed to descend to a depth of 850 feet. With some modifications, it could possibly descend to 1800 feet. We never anticipated a recovery in a diving bell at this depth."

"When could the ship be ready for sea?" the admiral asked.

"It is scheduled to be completed early next year. We can have her ready for sea in about four or five weeks with addition funds and shipyard workers working around the clock," the commander replied. "I would like to point out the problems involved. Lowering that bell to that depth and attaching it to the access hatch of the sunken hull is like trying to thread a needle with your eyes closed. It's never been attempted. The research vehicle Telstar IV can be used to guide the bell in place as it approaches the hull. If anyone has any other recommendations, I'd be glad to incorporate them in the rescue plan."

"You have approval to proceed with your plan," the admiral said. "There will be no press release on the results of this conference. SUBMISS alert is still in effect. SUBSUNK is to remain classified until further notice."

The conference was adjourned. Most of the officers departed, some quickly and others slowly. A few remained including Commander Hill and the admiral.

"Gentlemen I have some additional information that you should know, and I need your recommendations. This information is released on a strict need to know basis which includes only you in this room," the admiral stated with a grim look. "Intelligence has informed us that the Soviets have intercepted our communications with *(Redacted).* They plan to dispatch a sortie of ships south from the Baltic to the recovery area. The ships include a highly experienced submarine salvage vessel. The salvage vessel is carrying one of two advanced DSRV developed by the Soviet Union. We have known for some time that the Soviets are well ahead of us in the development of deep-sea rescue vessels. As you well know, they have had several submarines lost in recent years. As a result, they rapidly increased their efforts in deep sea rescue. The Pentagon has stated that they want to avoid an armed conflict at all costs. Hopefully the Soviets will fail in the efforts to board *(Redacted)* or salvage her."

"Are you saying that the plan is do nothing?" asked Commander Hill.

"Unfortunately, that is the only option at this time. If the Soviets arrive and commence recovery operations in international waters, we are ordered to stand down," the admiral replied. "I tried very hard to convince them to reconsider and take a more forceful stance. I am not a politician and I guess I was out of my league. They are steadfast in their decision. Based upon the timetable you have provided; I doubt if we can complete our recovery efforts before they arrive."

Commander Hill hesitated for a moment and replied, "My recommendation, Admiral, would be to dispatch Task Force Delta to intercept and delay the Soviet salvage sortie for as long as possible. I don't believe the Soviets would provoke a confrontation until we have a chance to talk. If preliminary talks fail, we could then withdraw the Task Force south and form a blockade north of the recovery area. I would think that it would take them awhile to decide that we have no intention of violating International Law and stopping their salvage operations in international waters. A task force of one carrier, several cruisers and destroyers accompanied by a group of submarines would at least scare the hell of them. Best case scenario would be that they would simply turn around and go home. It could buy us some time and give our guys a chance to get the crew out and destroy the remains of *(Redacted)*. We certainly don't yet have the capability to salvage *(Redacted)* at that depth."

"Very well, Commander," replied the admiral. "Demolition of the hull is not an option since we know that we have survivors down there. I will pass your recommendation with my approval to the Pentagon. This meeting is adjourned gentlemen. Art… would you stay behind for a moment?"

"Yes Admiral, something else you need for me to do?" the commander asked after everyone left the room.

"No, Art. I just wanted to say goodbye. I've received orders to Westpac Naval Supply Depot in Subic Bay, Philippines. I am to be in charge of Seventh Fleet Logistics. They're kicking me topside to the surface fleet with a thank you for your service. Guess they just want to get rid of a pain in their ass. Pissed them off dearly when the *Thresher* went down. I raised holy hell when I lost additional funding for the DSRV. Should have kept my mouth shut on this one."

"You did what you knew was right," the commander replied. "You couldn't just all but abandon those guys down there without a fight."

"I lost all credibility when I urged the Joint Chiefs to pull our submarines out of the war zone when Israel attacked. I guess you can pick and choose when it's a political war. Can't change what's been done," the admiral remarked. "I'll give your recommendation to send Task Force Delta as a diversion my best shot. They can't fire me since they already have," the admiral said with a big smile. "Think I'll hold off on my retirement for a while. A change to the far east just might be good for me. Get in some sun and beach time. Good luck, Art."

The admiral shook his hand as the commander just nodded, lowered his head and went out the door.

Construction on the new rescue ship was accelerated. The coordinated efforts of all departments of the Navy were brought to bear on the common effort. The true meaning of the situation was realized by all. What couldn't possibly happen had happened. When human life was actually placed in the balance, values and priorities quickly shifted. Human nature remained true to form.

Several days later Commander Hill received a call from the office of ComSubLant. "Commander Hill…this is Admiral Chase's staff officer. I just wanted to let you know that your recommendation to deploy the task force as a diversion has been approved. Admiral Chase is now the deputy commander. He sends his regrets that he could not call and will be in touch at a later date."

"Have the rules of engagement been modified or stand down orders to remain in effect?" the commander asked.

"Commander, that's all I am at liberty to say on this unsecured line," the officer replied. "I do have a message from Admiral Bentley sent before his departure. He said to tell you, *I did my best but only won half the battle. Hope your recommendation will be enough.*"

"Thanks for the call," the commander replied. "Gave my regards to Admiral Chase."

"*Half is better than nothing, I'll put that in the win column,*" he thought.

SubSunk-111 Days

The wind-blown ocean waves rose and fell in an irregular pattern. The rescue ship, *Sunbird,* rode over the crest of the waves; occasionally listing heavy to one side before righting itself and straining against its anchor chain. A red marker buoy floated just astern marking the approximate location of the sunken hull.

A mere 1800 feet below the surface, six men waited for the moment they would be free. Each day was much like the last without much assurance that tomorrow would be any different. The only cohesive force, hope, was quickly dwindling away. Each man retreated into his own world of memories or fantasies.

Lee spent most of his time sitting on the deck leaning against the bulkhead with his arms folded staring into space. He had become more and more withdrawn. He seldom spoke to anyone except in a heated argument. His beard had grown long and tangled. He refused to bathe or stand a watch. For some reason he blamed his companions for all his problems and hated them intensely.

White's easy-going attitude had almost completely disappeared. He remained apart from the rest of the men most of the time. His occasional conversations were limited to stories about his wife and child which he had told repeatedly.

Franklin was the most bitter of all. He should have already received his discharge from the Navy. He constantly reminded the others that he shouldn't be there.

Robishaw did his best to lighten the atmosphere. He told stories of his time as a shrimp boat crew member out of New Orleans and the times he rode out hurricanes at sea. No one would have guessed that he was an able-bodied seaman. After a while he also became withdrawn and quiet.

Lieutenant Eddy's death had a lasting effect on Corbett. He wandered about the compartments like a caged animal. He seldom volunteered to assume any responsibility. The necessary leadership factor was now absent.

Other men have experienced many hardships enduring the pains of wounds and loneliness. They survived and died demonstrating exceptional bravery and cowardice. Each experience could be described as unique. The actions of the survivors of the *(Redacted)* should only be judged in the total irony of their situation. Less than a half mile from safety, they could only wait and hope. The strain of uncertainty had indeed taken its toll.

The date is 4 May 1968. *Sunbird* on been on station and anchored 1800 feet above (Redacted) for about 35 days. Onboard *Sunbird* Banyan picked up ICQ telephone and called. "*(Redacted)* this is *Sunbird*, over."

Corbett picked up the microphone and answered. "Go ahead *Sunbird*."

"This is Banyan speaking. The rescue ship *Pigeon* will be here tomorrow. We'll be making the rescue attempt as soon as possible."

"It can't be too soon," Corbett replied. "This is a nice place to visit, but I wouldn't want to live here."

"I'm glad you still have a sense of humor," Banyan returned. "You should be glad you're not up here. It's raining cats and dogs."

"Very funny," Corbett said with a rare smile.

"The two-man surveillance mini sub arrived on station yesterday. Before the rescue ship arrives, we'll be taking photographs of the hull so see you soon."

"You're just a bundle of laughs today, Mister Banyan. You wouldn't consider giving me a ride back with you, would you?"

Banyan's voice became serious. "I wish I could, Sailor. I wish I could." He felt that he should change the subject. "What are you going to do with all the back pay you have coming when you get out?"

"Back pay, gosh. I don't know. I haven't thought about it."

"Think about it now."

"I guess I'll go on leave. I think I'd like to get married."

"What's your girl's name?"

"Nonie," Corbett replied with a smile. "She's a senior in college."

"I understand you're going to college. How do you feel about becoming an officer?"

Corbett lowered his head and remained silent.

"Are you still there, Corbett?" Banyan asked.

"I'm here," Corbett replied quickly. "I'm afraid getting a commission is out of the question now. I'll be lucky if they let me stay in the Navy."

"What do you mean?"

"I'll tell you someday when I get out of here. Until then, it's best to let it be. What happens on (**Redacted**) stays on (**Redacted**)," Corbett replied.

"Just as you say," Banyan said. "I have to make the final checks for the dive now. I'll call you later."

"Good luck. This is *(Redacted)*, out," Corbett replied as he turned off the UQC underwater telephone and replaced the microphone.

On the surface, Banyan and Page completed the final preparations for the descent to determine the exact location and photograph the sunken hull. The mini sub arrived from the west coast transported aboard aircraft to Norfolk and then a salvage support vessel to the recovery site.

They crawled into the Telstar in a prone position and the hatch was closed. The small submarine was then lowered from the stern of the rescue ship. After slowly moving away from the mother ship at short distance, it disappeared beneath the surface.

The search lights on the bow of the vessel reached only ten feet ahead in the darkness of the ocean depths. Schools of fish darted quickly from its path avoiding the unexpected brightness.

"Increase speed to three knots," Banyan ordered as he operated the depth control levers.

Page increased the speed on the small battery powered motors. "Depth 300 feet. You'd better reverse direction. We're getting too far to the west of the estimated position."

Banyan banked the small submarine to right and commenced a spiraling course downward to the ocean depths. An hour later they were approached by the ocean floor. The cramped space was becoming very cold.

"We'd better reduce speed, Vic, before we pile up on something."

"No, I want to cover as much ground as possible," Banyan replied. "We have to ascend in a couple of hours. Let go the amidships ballast."

Page released a lead weight below the sub allowing it to achieve neutral buoyancy and slowing its descent. The two men strained their eyes as they peered through the view ports at the bow. They searched for many minutes along a path of visibility five feet wide and ten feet ahead without success.

"We've got to get lower," Banyan said as he pushed the control lever forward. "We can't see a damn thing up here."

"I hope you know what you're doing," Page remarked.

"You watch for obstacles ahead and I'll search the bottom," Banyan replied.

The sub descended slowly, and the bottom became clearly visible a few feet below them. A small sea creature burrowed its way through the mud ahead and veered quickly off to the left as it was struck by the bright light. The current created by the vehicle's propeller churned up the mud on the bottom and engulfed the small sub in a dark cloud of silt.

"We've got to get back up a little," Page said. "We're stirring up too much mud. I can't see a blasted thing."

Banyan pulled back on the control lever and brought the mini sub slowly upward. The view cleared as it ascended.

"What's that?" Banyan asked as he slid forward in his position in order to see more clearly.

"It's some sort of container buried in the mud," Page replied. "Look, there's a piece of metal to the right. We must be getting close. We…look out! Rock ahead!" he shouted.

A large sharp rock loomed just ahead of them. Banyan quickly pulled the control lever back and turned the sub sharply to the right. They held their breath in anxious anticipation as the mini sub glided past the obstacle. A sharp jolt suddenly shook the small craft as it struck the pinnacle. The rock scraped down the side and hit the small propeller. The overhead and search lights went out momentarily as the shaft stopped, but slowly returned as they cleared the rock. The small shaft made a loud squealing noise as it turned. Water poured in around the shaft packing gland.

"Tighten down on that packing gland," Banyan shouted as he cut the power and allowed the sub to slowly settle to the bottom.

Page quickly tightened down on the shaft packing gland. "Leakage is stopped," he said as he crawled back to the bow. "Water level in the bilge is okay, no danger to the equipment."

Banyan energized the propulsion power and brought the sub slowly off the bottom. "We can't get over a knot of speed with that damaged shaft. Five minutes more and we head for the surface."

The mini sub followed the trail of scattered debris which became denser as they traveled east. The black hull of the sunken submarine suddenly appeared just ahead.

"There she is," Page said shaking Banyan's shoulder vigorously.

"I see it," Banyan replied. "Check out the camera equipment."

The drifting mud had piled up on the sides of the sunken hull like a sand dune in the desert. The sail area and diving planes protruded upward like the head and wings of an eagle just inside their range of vision. It appeared sinister and proud, but very dead.

"We'll go up the port side around the bow and down the starboard side," Banyan said. "Turn on the stand-by lighting and start photographing when you're ready."

"Alright," Page replied. "We haven't got much time left."

"We'll take the time," Banyan returned.

The small submarine traveled around the sunken hull like a baby whale nudging its mother. A large gaping hole on the starboard side of the bow stood as evidence to the fateful tragedy. As they passed the outside of the engineering compartment, a sign of life within appeared. The discharge of warm water from (**Redacted**)*'s* steam condenser was being expelled from a hull opening. The stream of water cut a path through the mud and formed a cloud which drifted up and slowly disappeared in the darkness.

Banyan's thoughts were quickly transferred to the trapped sailors inside. "Poor devils," he mumbled.

"We just might join them," Page said, "if we don't start back up. Our air supply and battery power are running low."

"I guess you're right," Banyan returned. "Let go all ballast. We've done all we can."

The lead weights along the bottom of the small sub were discarded and it began to ascend quickly toward the surface. In several minutes it broke the surface of the water five miles astern of the rescue ship.

"Release the green flare and the marker buoy," Banyan ordered.

The rescue ship quickly headed in the direction of the flare and the Telstar was hoisted back aboard.

Banyan inspected the damage to Telstar and discovered that the shaft was severely bent. Repairs would have to be made before the next dive. To add to their problems the weather conditions were getting worse. The wind was picking up and the rain came down even harder.

Part Four: Above and Beyond

SitRep 8-Common Virtue/Uncommon Valor
SubSunk-112 Days

The date is 5 May 1968. Late that afternoon, the rescue ship *Pigeon*, arrived on station several days ahead of schedule. The rescue attempt was planned for sunrise the next day.

The weather had become progressively worse during the night. The following morning the two rescue ships were being tossed about on the high waves. The ships would momentarily disappear from sight of one another in the see-saw action of the deep swells.

Telstar had been repaired and was ready for the descent. Banyan was selected to pilot it while Page would descend in the diving bell. Banyan decided that he didn't want to put anyone else at risk as co-pilot of the Telstar.

They stood at the stern of the *Sunbird* while the crew lowered the small boat which would transfer Page to *Pigeon*.

"You be careful, buddy," Banyan said. "The weather is getting worse. You just say the word and we'll call it off."

"No, we've got to give it a try," Page remarked. "Those guys down there can't take it much longer."

"I thought you'd say that. Good luck and I'll call you on the underwater telephone once we're submerged."

"See you later," Page replied with a handshake as he climbed on the side of the ship and jumped into the small boat.

The small boat sped away climbing the crest of the waves on his way to *Pigeon*. The spray of salt water drenched its passengers. It quickly disappeared from sight and could only be seen occasionally as it reappeared atop a wave in the distance.

Banyan stood and watched for a long time before he turned and walked to the stern of the ship to make the final preparations aboard Telstar.

He felt very much alone as they closed the access hatch of the vehicle and lowered it to the water. Piloting the small craft, a short distance away, he submerged to a shallow depth and circled waiting for the diving bell to be launched.

On board the *Pigeon*, the large orange diving bell was lowered by cable beneath the ship between the two pontoons of the catamaran. An umbilical cord supplied air from the ship to the bell.

"*Pigeon* this is Telstar. How do you hear me, John?" Banyan called.

"I hear you loud and clear Telstar."

"I hear you same. Is everything okay?"

"Conditions normal," Page replied.

The men in *(Redacted)* huddled in silence around their underwater telephone and listened to the two-way conversation.

"Let's take it slow and easy," Banyan said. "I'm heading in your direction. You should pick me up visually in a few minutes."

The bell was lowered slowly and Banyan piloted Telstar downward to a rendezvous.

"Depth 200 feet... how are you doing, John?"

"Everything is normal so far. The wave action on the ship is jerking my cable pretty hard," Page replied.

"Keep a close eye on your strain gage. If the tension on the cable goes too high, call it quits and we'll head back up."

"Don't worry, ole man," Page returned. "It'll be okay."

"Just do as I say…okay, buddy?"

"I can see your lights just above me on a bearing of two-six-five degrees," Page said peering through one of his portholes. "Continue on your present course and rate of descent."

"I think I see your lights," Banyan returned. "Good to see you again."

"Same here," Page returned. "I'm increasing my rate of descent."

The cable aboard *Pigeon* began to reel out faster lowering the bell to the ocean depths. Banyan piloted Telstar in a circling motion following it on downward.

"Depth 1,000 feet," Banyan called. "How much cable do you have out?"

"2,000 feet," Page answered.

"The current is driving you to the northeast."

"Yes, I know," Page replied. "I'll have *Pigeon* change station and reposition me back over the hull."

"What does your strain gage read?"

Page looked on the gage mounted near the overhead of the bell. The needle stood a short distance from the red danger area. "It's okay," he said.

"What does it read?" Banyan repeated.

"90 percent," Page replied.

"That's cutting it pretty close, John. The current is pushing you more than we expected. The pull to reposition you could part your cable."

"No turning back now, buddy," Page said. "Here's where I see if I live right."

"John, what are you doing?"

Page did not answer but picked up another microphone with direct communications with the rescue ship. "*Pigeon* this is Warrant Officer Page. Request you change station 1,000 yards to the south."

A voice returned over his speaker. "This is *Pigeon*… will do."

The rescue ship began to slowly move to the southeast pulling the bell suspended beneath it. Page stood and watched the needle of the gage as it slowly moved into the red danger area.

"John, this is Vic. I'm giving you a direct order to abort the dive and head for the surface." He waited but received no answer. "John, did you hear what I said?" he called again.

"I hear you, Vic. Don't worry. It's…"

The transmission was interrupted by a loud blast.

Banyan slid forward in his small craft looking out his view ports. He caught a glimpse of the orange bell as it fell quickly through the beam of his search lights and disappeared in the darkness below.

A broken transmission came over his speaker. "Cable parted…flooding…down"

"John!" Banyan shouted gripping his microphone tightly and staring into the emptiness below.

Onboard *(Redacted)*, White grabbed Corbett's shoulder and shook it vigorously. "What's happening?" he asked.

"Be quiet and listen," Corbett replied shoving him away. "I think they've lost the diving bell."

"Oh, my God," White said slowly lowering his head.

Banyan lay motionless a long time. He let the microphone drop from his hand and lowered his head to rest on his forearm. He held back his grief. "You stupid son-of-a-bitch," he said suddenly grabbing to control the lever and pulling it all the way back.

The Telstar nosed upward and headed toward the surface.

"*Pigeon* this is Telstar, over."

A voice returned over his speaker, "What's going on down there? The cable is reeling in slack."

"The cable and mechanism parted," Banyan replied. "Warrant Officer Page is gone. The diving bell is down below its crush depth. I'm coming up."

Silence pervaded.

"Roger, Telstar," the voice replied.

"*(Redacted)*, this is Telstar, over."

Corbett picked up his microphone. "This is *(Redacted)*. We heard, Mister Banyan. I'm sorry."

"I'll call you later when I'm back aboard, Corbett," Banyan returned.

"I understand. This is *(Redacted)*, out," Corbett replied as he turned off the underwater telephone. He stood up slowly and walked silently away from the others. After a moment Franklin and Lee also stood and walked away leaving White alone. He still sat with his head lowered and began to sob.

Later that day Banyan called. "(**Redacted**) this is *Sunbird,* over."

Corbett picked up the UQC. "This is Corbett, go ahead."

"This is Banyan. The weather is getting worse up here. A tropical depression is heading this way. It's expected to get much worse within twenty-four hours. We have to get underway to evade the storm."

"When will you be back?"

"It's hard to say. It could be three or four days."

"You don't sound very convincing," Corbett returned. "It could be even longer, couldn't it?"

After a pause, Banyan replied. "Yes, it could. Another depression is forming further to the south."

There was a pause for a few moments.

"Don't be discouraged. Another diving bell will be on its way. We'll be back and get you out of there."

"Give it to me straight, Mister Banyan. Is there any hope?"

After another pause, Banyan replied slowly. "There's always hope, Jim."

"Yeah, there's always hope," Corbett said as he flipped off the UQC power switch.

Later that evening, the atmosphere aboard *(**Redacted**)* was a solemn one. The men were quiet and spoke only when absolutely necessary. They had avoided discussing the day's events as long as possible. Sooner or later they would have to realize the full impact of their situation.

White had fully recovered from his encounter with Lee and was on watch in maneuvering when an alarm sounded along with a flashing red light. "What the hell is that?" White shouted.

Corbett rushed into maneuvering. "That's a reactor compartment high radiation alarm. We must have a primary coolant leak. What is the level in the pressurizer?"

"Reading 75% and dropping slowly," White replied quickly. "That's not good. That's not good at all."

"I'm going to the reactor compartment tunnel and see if I can locate the leak," Corbett said as he hurried forward to the reactor compartment. "Come with me, Elvis."

The two men reached the reactor compartment tunnel and Corbett peered through the glass porthole into the reactor compartment. Steam filled the compartment and it was difficult to see every part of the room.

"I think I see the leak," Corbett said. "The primary coolant sampling station piping appears to be ruptured."

Water under 1,000 psi of pressure and 350 degrees gushed from the small ruptured pipe and flashed to steam. The radioactive steam cooled and fell like foggy rain to the reactor compartment deck.

"What's the worst-case scenario that we are looking at here Corbett?" Ellsworth asked.

"Not sure if the primary water supply make up pump can keep up with the water loss," Corbett replied.

"I'm not a qualified nuke so that means what?"

"If that happens, the reactor core is uncovered without cooling water and we have a major core melt down," Corbett replied. "At that point we're all just feed for the fishes you might say. The only other alternative is we could just shut down the reactor and die when the oxygen runs out or until the bilge water fills the compartments."

"So, what in the hell do you think we can do?"

"What I plan to do is suit up with as much radiation shielding that I can carry and close that isolation valve for the piping leading to the sampling station," Corbett replied.

"That can be pretty dangerous can't it? The radiation level in that compartment is pretty high and will only get higher," Ellsworth continued.

"Yes! That is very true. I would say that I will get a RAD dose much more that my lifetime allowable limit," Corbett replied.

 "What you mean without actually saying is that you will probably die?" Ellsworth asked with a frown on his face.

"I'm pretty hard to kill but we shall see. Can't say for sure but I do know that the NRC will never allow me to work around reactors any more that's for sure. I would say seriously that is the least of my worries," Corbett returned with a surprising grin. "If you have any other ideas, I'd love to hear them."

"Yeah, I have a better idea," he replied. "I suit up and I go in and I close that valve."

Corbett looked at him with a puzzled look. "No, Elvis. I would never order anyone to do anything that I would not do myself."

"You are not ordering me to do it," he replied with a stern look. "I'm saying that I should do it. I am the most logical person to do it. When it comes to doing what has to be done around here, I'm as useless as tits on a boar hog when compared to you. I do know how to close a simple valve. You are the last person we can lose, and you know that is a fact."

Corbett lowered his head in deep thought for few moments. "Elvis, I am proud to be your shipmate. You can't argue with logic like that. Let's get you suited up. If you change your mind or have second thoughts at any time, I want to know."

"Won't do any good for you to change your mind," Ellsworth replied. "You can't stop me from going in and it doesn't take two of us to close one valve."

Corbet merely smiled and shook his head in agreement as the two men quickly moved from the reactor compartment tunnel to the machinery space. Corbett helped him as he put on the white radiation suit. Franklin joined them as they worked.

"What the hell is going on?" Franklin asked.

"Elvis is going into the reactor compartment and shut the isolation valve to the primary coolant sampling station piping. That is the location of the primary system leak," Corbett replied.

"But the radiation level is above allowable limits in there," Franklin remarked. "There's no boron shielding on the reactor vessel at that location not to mention the contaminated primary cooling water everywhere. This is crazy. It's reading above 500R/hr. A reading of 200 R is essentially a death sentence."

Corbett kept working and did not reply.

Ellsworth just looked at Franklin and smiled.

Franklin lowered his head for a few moments. He reached over and grabbed Ellsworth pulling him into his arms. He surprising hugged him tightly. Seemed like a long time before Franklin pushed him back and said, "You get in there, shut that goddamn valve and get the hell out, Sailor. I would say that you only have a few minutes. Don't make me have to come in and drag your ass out."

"Will do, Sir," he replied.

The men proceeded to the access hatch in the reactor compartment tunnel leading to the reactor below. Corbett opened the hatch, Ellsworth entered and climbed down the access ladder. Corbett and Franklin watched through the window in the reactor compartment tunnel.

Ellsworth headed quickly to the source of the leak at the sample station. Several inches of steaming water covered the reactor compartment deck. Radioactive steam was pouring from the ruptured piping. The heat from the escaping steam was starting to burn his skin inside his suit. His body was drenched with sweat. He found the isolation valve and tried to turn it shut. The valve wheel would not move. He struggled with the valve for several minutes without success. He stumbled back and fell to his knees exhausted. The high radiation coming from the primary system cooling water and reactor vessel penetrated his body making his muscles weaker and weaker. He grabbed a wrench from his utility belt and struggled to his feet. He put the wrench around the valve stem and pulled down with all his strength. The valve refused to turn.

Robishaw entered the reactor compartment tunnel. "How's he doing so far?"

"Can't get the damn isolation valve shut," Franklin replied.

Robishaw looked through the tunnel window into the reactor compartment. "He can't get the valve shut. Is there a backup isolation valve?" he asked.

"The backup isolation valve is there on the opposite bulkhead labeled PS-158 but I don't think he can get...," Franklin attempted to reply.

"It's our only chance. He needs help," Robishaw interrupted. "The leak seems to be getting much worse."

Without hesitation Robishaw lifted the access hatch and quickly dropped down the ladder into the reactor compartment. He didn't take the time to put on radiation protection gear which would have actually been of little or no help.

"What the hell are you doing, Robby?" Franklin shouted.

"He's doing what he knows has to be done," Corbett replied.

Robishaw waded through the ankle-deep water to reach the backup isolation valve. He was not very tall and unable to reach the valve high on the bulkhead. He looked around but could not find anything to stand on to reach the valve. He removed his belt from his pants, folded it and threw it up and over the valve stem to make a sling. He pulled himself up the bulkhead to a point where he could reach the valve. He was able to close the valve easily even though it was burning and blistering his hand.

The steam from the ruptured pipe at the sampling station trickled to a stop.

Ellsworth had collapsed unconscious to the deck. Robishaw managed to drag him to the ladder leading to the tunnel access hatch. He lifted him up the ladder as Franklin reached and pulled him up into the tunnel.

Robishaw then struggled to climb the ladder leading out of the reactor compartment as Corbett reached down the ladder and pulled him out. He rested on the tunnel deck exhausted.

"Would you say that I got it done, Capt'n?" Robishaw asked.

"That you did," Corbett answered with a big smile. "That you did, buddy."

Corbett and Franklin rushed to remove the wet and contaminated clothing of the two men. They could see that both had blistered and pealing skin from the high radiation that had penetrated their bodies. Both men were unconscious with an extremely high pulse rate.

"They seem to be in shock. We have to get them back to the engine room," Corbett ordered.

The men did their best to make their shipmates comfortable since that was all they could do. Robishaw's pulse became weaker and weaker as he expelled fluids from all parts of his body and became increasingly dehydrated. Thankfully he often became unconscious as the pain emanating from his entire body became unbearable. It was a terrible death which finally came in a few days. His final words were "Tell my dad…" He was unable to finish expressing his final thoughts.

Remarkably Ellsworth lived a few days longer before he also passed.

White walked into the maneuvering room with Corbett and dropped to his blanket bed on the deck. "I'm out of shape," he stated as he raised and lowered his arms and then his legs to relieve the stiffness. "I need to run some laps and lift some weights maybe."

"So, how's the head?" Corbet asked.

"No problem. Almost as good as new," he replied.

"Have you noticed any nausea or any other stomach issues…like maybe…diarrhea?" Corbett asked with a concerned look. "Have you had any hair loss?"

"No. None of that. I'm just getting over the shits though. Why would you ask?"

"Francis has these symptoms. I do to some extent," Corbett replied as he ran his hand through his thick dark hair. "I would say that we may have internal radiation exposure. It seems like you and Lee are okay for now."

"What the hell? So, what is going to happen?"

"Your guess is as good mine I would say," Corbett replied. "I don't think that we'll experience the same fate as Elvis and Robby, at least not in the near term. More than likely we were exposed to internal alpha radiation when we helped the guys out of the reactor compartment."

White looked down as he spoke quietly. "So that means that it will just take longer to kill you I guess."

"That's possible but just not sure. Guess we should have been more careful disposing of their contaminated clothing. What's done is done," Corbett remarked with a grim look.

"I assume that Francis and Lee know about what you just told me?" White asked.

"Yes. We've had this same discussion. Lee is fine. No symptoms. Francis, you know Francis. It takes a lot to get him upset."

The two men sat silently and looked at one another with nothing more to say.

Ellsworth and Robishaw had died rather quickly from high energy gamma and beta radiation that penetrated their bodies like bullets. Corbett and Franklin were likely exposed to low energy alpha particles that enter the body like a virus and slowly attack and damage the vital organs. Chances are Lee and White are safe for the time being. The damaged reactor which they need for survival is slowly contaminating the small world in which they live. Just when you think matters can't get worse, they usually do. That's Murphy's Law.

SubSunk-122 Days

The date is 15 May 1968. After what seemed like an eternity to the men below, the rescue vessel returned to the red marker buoy. The men on *(Redacted)* have endured life aboard about the sunken submarine for 122 days.

Banyan called on the underwater telephone. *"(Redacted)*, this is *Sunbird*. *(Redacted)* this is *Sunbird*, over."

"This is *(Redacted)*," Corbett replied.

"We have a situation *(Redacted)*. We have just been informed by ComSubLant that there is a Soviet cruiser, two destroyers and a submarine salvage vessel steaming out of the Baltic south in route to this area. The salvage vessel is equipped with an advanced DSRV. It is obvious from intelligence gathered thus far that their mission is to either attempt to board *(Redacted)* or salvage and raise her to the surface."

Most of the message from *Sunbird* was garbled and suppressed by the many ocean sounds.

"*Sunbird* repeat your last more slowly," Corbett replied.

The message to *(Redacted)* was repeated several times slowly.

"I understand *Sunbird*. Any chance these guys will do a better job than you guys have done so far?" Corbett asked sarcastically.

"These guys know their stuff. They successfully salvaged one of their sunken submarines several months ago and almost rescued some of the crew. Things went south quickly, and they lost their crew and one of their two advanced DSRVs. Our assessment is that they are capable of pulling this off."

"Now that's nice to know," Corbett replied. "What the fuck are we supposed to do? What are you or should I say ComSubLant going to do? Pardon my language, Mr. Banyan but, as you can tell, I'm kinda pissed off right now."

"As I understand it, orders from the Pentagon are to avoid a conflict in the hopes that they will not succeed. Task Force Delta from the Sixth Fleet delayed the Soviet sortie of ships as long as possible. The Soviets are apparently aware that our rescue attempt has failed and that we do not have the capability to commence salvage operations to recover *(Redacted)*. The Soviets have decided to resume their boarding and salvage plans."

"Then what you are saying is the plan is to do nothing and let them take the boat and any of us that might still be alive."

"I would say that it was a difficult decision to make. We don't want the *(Redacted)* to fall into Soviet hands. You have highly classified electronic countermeasure equipment stored in the machinery space. But even more importantly, the Soviets will have intact all components of the RPJ propulsion system. If that happens, we will lose at least 10 years of a clear strategic submarine warfare advantage over the Soviets."

"You are saying is that it is up to us to do what we can to prevent them from getting their hands on *(Redacted)*," Corbett said sarcastically. "What in the hell do you propose? I have three crew members going apeshit down here. I am armed with one 45 caliber pistol and maybe two clips of ammunition. They have warships and I am sure they have a well-trained boarding party if that DSRV can get to us, which you say probably will."

The returned message from *Sunbird* over the UQC was short and again garbled as it was being drowned out by the surrounding array of natural ocean noises. Corbett listened as the echo of the transmission over the UQC slowly disappeared in the ocean depths. He stood at the UQC station for several minutes with his head lowered to his forearm trying to comprehend the situation. In frustration he slammed the microphone against the console several times before slowly sliding down the bulkhead and sat quietly on the deck. Another garbled message could be heard coming over the UQC. Corbett stood up, ran his hands slowly through his hair and tucked his shirt tail into his dungaree trousers. "*Sunbird* this is *(Redacted)*. Can you hear me, over?"

"I hear you *(Redacted)*," came clearly over the UQC.

"My name is Jim. What is your name?" Corbett asked.

"My name is Vic."

"May I call you Vic?" Corbett asked.

"Certainly, Jim." he replied. "This is no time for formalities."

"How much time do we have before these ass holes arrive?"

"ETA is in about seven days. They are steaming at max speed. Trying to make up some time since they were delayed," he replied.

"Is there any chance that the brass will change its mind and engage that sortie of ships?"

Banyan hesitated "You're asking a question that I cannot answer, Jim."

"I'll stick around as long as I can. I have been directed to stay within UQC range to see if they get their DSRV attached to your machinery space hatch."

"You should know, I'm damn sure as hell not going to give up without a fight. We can delay them at the topside entrance hatch to the machinery space and then at the watertight door to the engineering compartment. After that…we will see," Corbett stated with determination in his voice. "We can at least surprise the shit out of them if only for a little while." The echo of the transmission verberated against the ocean current as it traveled to the surface.

"I have no direct orders to pass on regarding what you should do, Jim. I was not even told to inform you about the Soviet salvage attempt," Banyan stated. "I am certain that it would not reflect badly on you or your shipmates if you just did nothing."

"So why in the hell would ComSubLant want to keep us in the dark? There is one thing I do know for sure," Corbett replied. "Captain Flynn would not give up the boat to a bunch of fuck'n Soviets lying down without a fight. I am senior petty officer on board which makes me the commanding officer of the *(Redacted)* until I am relieved. Am I right or am I wrong, Warrant Officer Banyan?"

"Affirmative Petty Officer Corbett," Banyan replied. "Good luck, Sailor. You're going to need it. Give me a shout out if there is anything I can do which I am sure is nothing."

"Can you give me an update on our status at home? Have the families been notified yet? What have they been told? I have guys down here that have been wondering," Corbett asked.

Banyan hesitated for a few moments and replied, "*(Redacted)* is still being reported as failing to arrive from an extended deployment, assumed lost at sea and whereabouts unknown at this time. Locating *(Redacted)* and your situation have not been disclosed and classified Secret for obvious reasons."

"What can I say? Fuck it!" Corbett returned rather confused. "Good luck with that bullshit story you're feeding the public. I guess that means that we can't get messages to our families or friends."

After a short pause Banyan replied, "I don't think that would be possible, Jim."

"I guess that tells me everything I need to know. See you on the other side wherever that may be, Vic. This is *(Redacted)*, out"

Corbett went to maneuvering where Franklin was standing watch. "Average temperature in the reactor is very low, Francis. We're losing steam pressure. You need to bring it up a little," Corbett ordered.

"You don't have to tell me. I was about to do that. I know what I'm doing," he replied as he slowly moved the reactor rod control rod switch to the raise position. The power level in the nuclear reactor increased and increased the water temperature circulating through the reactor and the steam generators.

"Just be careful, Francis. Don't want the generators to trip on slow speed and trip the breakers," Corbett replied sternly. "So, get your head out of your ass and pay attention."

"I need for you guys to listen up," Corbett ordered. "I think you all heard and know the situation. Soon the Soviets ships are going to be on our ass, and we have a lot to do to get ready. I do not intend to just give up the ship. We are not going to make it easy for them."

"What the hell do you mean, Corbett? What can we do?" Lee asked. "Don't we get a say in this?"

"I am senior man on board," Corbett replied. "I have the responsibility to protect this boat to the best of my ability. Higher ups have apparently given up and washed their hands of the situation. I guess they expect us to just sit on our ass and do nothing hoping they will not be able to get to us or the boat. I have received no orders one way or the other. I can order you to do as I say but under the circumstances not sure if you'll comply. You guys can speak your mind. I know what I plan to do, and I hope that all of you will give me hand."

"I say we take a short ride topside in that Soviet DSRV if it can get to us," Lee interrupted. "We'll spend a while being interrogated and then they'll probably let us go or maybe trade us for some high-level spy or something like that. I hear they do that kind of shit."

"You can bet your sweet ass that I plan to make it as hard as hell for them to get aboard this boat. Not only because of the classified equipment and machinery onboard but also, I don't trust those assholes to ever let us go. We made fools out of them, disabled three of their merchant ships, sunk one of their destroyers and killed a bunch of their sailors."

"You let us know what you have in mind," Franklin interrupted. "I am with you, Corbett, as far as I can go. Not sure how far that will be…like to the very end. Whatever that may be."

"Thanks. Hope it won't be that far, shipmate," Corbett replied.

"We'll bring up several cylinders of oxygen and welding acetylene from the lower level. We'll put the oxygen and acetylene together at the bottom of the access hatch from topside and at the watertight door coming from the auxiliary machinery space to the engine room. We have to come up with a way to set them off as they come through," Corbett explained. "Hopefully the first blast as they come down the hatch will scare them off for good, but I doubt it."

"Let's hope the explosion doesn't rupture the hull," Franklin explained with a frown.

"Don't think it will but if it does our worries will be over. If I remember my chemistry and welding class right, it should be a small explosion and mostly fire," Corbett explained. "If the pressure hull does go, maybe they won't be so lucky with their salvage operations."

"If we can't stop them from getting to us, what then?" White asked.

"We'll have to wait until that happens," Corbett replied with a confused look. "Haven't thought that far ahead yet."

"Francis give me a hand getting the gas cylinders up from below. White take over in maneuvering. Lee, you can help if you want. If not, just keep the fuck out of our way," Corbett ordered sternly.

Franklin hesitated before he spoke, "Corbett, I have a favor to ask."

"Yes, Francis. What is it?"

Franklin looked down as he spoke. "I have a bad feeling about what is about to happen. If I don't make it out of here, would you let Snell's family know that I am very sorry about what happened? I wasn't drunk like they say."

"I understand, Francis. We're all getting out of here so don't worry."

"I want to say, just so you know, Corbett we met up with Doc that night on the movie run. I only had one drink of his medical alcohol mixed with something. Didn't taste that good to me and I always feel like shit when I drink at all. Snell had more to drink than he should. He and Doc were swapping shots. Snell had been driving but I took over for him. I dropped Doc at some night club just before the accident. It was dark as hell and I got lost. I was driving a little too fast because we were late getting back. I saw something dart across the road in front of me, so I swerved off the road. I would give anything if it had me that didn't make it out of that damn ditch. That's the absolute true story, so help me God."

"I believe you, Frank. We have things to do so let's get it done."

"I'll help," Lee remarked.

That was the first time Franklin had mentioned anything to anyone about the circumstances surrounding the automobile accident that killed Seaman Snell. Not one of his shipmates had asked. They knew Franklin would tell his story when he was ready.

SubSunk-129 Days

The date is 22 May 1968. The Soviet ships arrived at the sight of the sunken submarine as expected. Active sonar from the salvage vessel quickly located the hull of **(Redacted)** as it mapped the surrounding ocean floor and the remnants of the sunken submarine. The men below could only sit and listen to the constant pinging of the sonar of the vessel overhead.

The Soviet DSRV was quickly prepared for its dive and lowered over the side of the rescue vessel with three operators inside. The DSRV was tossed around in the rough sea for several minutes and then quickly submerged on its way to the submarine below. The *Sunbird* was on station several miles away on the horizon and observed the actions of the sortie of ships surrounding the site.

The men below could hear the faint sounds of screws of the DSRV as it circled the sunken hull. Next came the clanging of metal to metal as the DSRV attempted to mate with the access hatch above the machinery space. The first attempt failed and the DSRV circled the sunken hull for a second try.

"They don't seem to be having much luck," Corbett stated. "Maybe they won't be able to attach to the access hatch."

"Not sure if that is a good or bad thing," Lee replied. "Still seems kinda stupid to hope that our only way out of here doesn't work."

"You have a short memory, Lee," Corbett said in angry tone. "You agreed with the plan with the rest of us. We are not going to just surrender and turn over the boat without a fight. If I still can't count on you Lee, just shut the hell up and stay out of the way."

"Wait a minute. Maybe we should talk about this some more," Franklin interrupted. "Let's see if they can make this happen. If they can, we can at least talk to them. Make a deal maybe."

"Make a deal? What the hell are you guys talking about? This damn discussion is over," Corbett replied.

"I'm with you all the way, Corbett," White spoke up with assurance. "You are in charge. You got us this far. No one else could have done it. We owe you our lives."

On the third attempt the crew of the DSRV was able to attach to the access hatch.

The crew of the DSRV quickly turned the wheel of the latching mechanism of the access hatch leading below.

As the access hatch flew opened, Corbett shouted, "Here they come. Get back to the engine room."

Lee, Franklin and Corbett hurried through the watertight door leading to the adjacent engine room. Corbett stood in the open door, pulled the 45-caliber pistol from his belt and fired two rounds as a man crawled down the ladder from the DSRV above. The man quickly climbed back up the ladder and closed the access hatch. After a few minutes, metal on metal sounds could be heard again as the Soviet DRSV broke away from the machinery space hatch and headed for the surface.

"Doubt if I hit anything but it sure scared the hell out of him," Corbett said with a grin. "Lee get the chainfall from the lower level. We'll hook it to the hatch and secure it to the overhead. Won't be able to open it so easy next time" Corbett explained. "I have a feeling they will be back pretty damn quick. This time they will be armed to teeth. I suspect that we will be faced with a pissed off boarding party."

"Oh shit!" Franklin replied. "I was hoping that you would not say that."

"We have no choice now," Corbett replied. "Let's just stick with the plan."

"Maybe you can talk to them over the UQC?" Lee asked. "Explain to them that we are ready to get the hell out of here."

"I don't speak Russian that well," Corbett replied. "I'm not ready to call it quits yet. I'll let you know when and if I decide to do that. Lee kill the lights in the machinery space and reactor compartment tunnel," Corbett ordered.

The Soviet DSRV was tossed about in the waves next to rescue vessel. A boarding party of seven or more heavily armed men climbed aboard the DSRV along with the three crew members. It quickly submerged on its way back down to the sunken submarine.

The DSRV shortly reached *(Redacted)* and mated again with the access hatch leading to the machinery space. This time the wheel of the latching mechanism on the access hatch would not turn. It was held shut tightly by the chain fall attached to hatch. Shortly sparks from a cutting torch could be seen falling from the access hatch. One by one the latching mechanisms and the chain fall fell to the deck below.

"Stay here and keep low," Corbett ordered as he hurried from the adjacent engine room to the ladder leading to the access hatch. He struggled for a moment as he tried to open the valves on the oxygen and welding acetylene cylinders. The gas could be heard as it slowly escaped from the cylinders and then quickly spread throughout the auxiliary machinery space.

Corbett quickly jumped through the open watertight door back to the engine room as the access hatch flew open. He had retrieved a flare gun from a metal cabinet nearby and waited cautiously just outside the watertight door leading to the machinery space.

Several men with night vision gear climbed down the ladder from the DSRV. Laser sights from their weapons spread around the dark compartment in all directions.

Corbett pointed the flare gun through the open door and fired. He quickly shut and dogged the watertight door. A trail of flaming red smoke spiraled forward into the gas filled compartment. The mixture of oxygen and welding acetylene exploded. Fragments of the gas cylinders and flames spread throughout the machinery space. The three men inside the compartment instinctively fired their weapons as they were engulfed in flames and cut down by the cylinder shrapnel. The men remaining in the DSRV were able to shut the vehicle access hatch in time and stay safe from the carnage below.

Corbett joined his shipmates in the maneuvering room. He slowly fell to his knees before rolling on his back and stared quietly at the overhead.

"Now what?" Franklin asked. "Don't think they're going to just turn tail and run now."

"I'm sure they don't intend to put up their hands surrender that's for sure." Corbett replied with a surprising grin. "I suppose that they'll come after us again after the fire in the machinery space burns out. Looks like the explosion took out the carbon dioxide removal system and oxygen generators. No air coming from the replenishing system ducts."

Lee stood up quickly at the reactor control panel. "I'll say it again. We should give it up," he said with a sense of desperation. "We've done all we can."

"I think I want to vote yes on that idea," Franklin added quickly.

"I know how you feel," Corbett replied. "What you are not considering is the fact that they probably don't give a shit what we want to do. They will certainly not take any risk trying to take us alive now."

Franklin sat quietly on the deck with his head lowered. He occasionally shook his head obviously agreeing with the hopelessness of the situation. "Crap…crap…and more crap," he mumbled to himself.

"Our only hope is to kill the rest of those son-of-a-bitches and disable the DSRV so they can't use it again," Corbett said sternly.

"So, what you are saying is with luck that puts us right back where we were before," Lee replied. "Stuck down here with no way out. I don't place any confidence in our guys being able to get us out of here."

In the machinery space the fire had burned out more quickly than anticipated and without the knowledge of the men huddled in the engine room. The remainder of the boarding party scurried down the ladder opened the watertight door leading to the engine room.

The only warning the group received was the watertight door opening and the clanging noise of a fragmentation grenade as it rolled across the compartment near the four men. Instinctively Franklin quickly threw himself on top of the grenade just as it detonated. He was lifted into the air by the explosion and fell lifeless to the deck.

Lee and Corbett dove to safety behind an electrical panel inside the maneuvering room along with White just as another grenade rolled across the compartment. Without hesitation White grabbed the grenade and ran toward the open watertight door. He reached the door and threw the grenade toward the men entering the compartment just as rounds from an automatic weapon struck him multiple times. He fell to the deck dead as the grenade exploded killing two men of the boarding party.

Without thinking Corbett stood up in an attempt to help his fallen friend. Surprisingly Lee quickly jumped in front of Corbett shielding him from a volley of gun fire. Lee was stuck first in the arm, then the neck and finally the chest. He fell wounded and bleeding to the deck.

From behind the electrical panel in the maneuvering room, Corbett quickly pulled and fired his meager 45-caliber pistol at the men armed with automatic weapons. He continued firing until his clip of ammunition was empty. His attacked was answered by a volley of shots that landed on the electrical panel protecting him. A smoke grenade was tossed inside the maneuvering room and quickly filled the area with smoke. He knew the next attack was soon to come.

The smoke engulfed Corbett as he held Lee in his arms. He saw immediately that there was nothing that could be done for him. "Sorry, buddy," Corbett said in low whisper.

Lee answered him by the only way he could. He held his hand tightly and smiled before he was engulfed by the pain of his wounds. As the pain subsided, Lee whispered, "Not bad for a worthless non-qualified nub loser…huh, Corbett?"

Instantly Corbett decided what he had to do. "What do you say, buddy? Let's send these bastards to hell," Corbett said with a slight grin.

Lee managed a smile and shook his head in agreement. His head then turned slowly to one side with his eyes staring at nothing.

Corbett moved quickly to the reactor control panel, grabbed the rod control switch and turned it to the full raise position. He withdrew the reactor control rods which first moved slowly but then gained speed as he held the switch in the raise position. The reactor power level quickly passed 100 percent power and the meter pegged just as Corbett flipped the high-power safety shutdown switch to the bypass position. He was protected by the smoke around him as rounds fired peppered the gages on the reactor control panel in front of him. With a look of pure determination beads of sweat poured down his face as he held the control rod switch tightly. The indicator lights went bright red as the reactor control rods reached the fully withdrawn position at the top of the reactor. At that point, Corbet knew his job was done. He smiled, released the rod control switch, sat on the deck next to the reactor control panel and waited for the inevitable. Nothing could be done now to stop what was coming.

Inside the reactor without the neutron absorbing control rods the nuclear fission process increased exponentially as more and more uranium atoms split apart converting mass to energy and releasing more neutrons to split even more uranium atoms. As the power level increased even higher, the temperature of the uranium metal fuel assemblies increased quickly above their designed limits. The cooling water in the reactor core circulating between the reactor vessel and steam generator began to boil. At first it was merely a trickle of bubbles forming along the sides of the many metal fuel assemblies and then slowly turning to steam.

On the subatomic particle level inside the nuclear reactor; slow moving delayed neutron particles from previous generations of the nuclear fission cycle, whose primary task were to keep the nuclear reactor under control, were quickly replaced by faster neutrons. Each generation of neutrons were faster and thus shorter lived than the last. The nuclear reactor now with its pulsating deep blue glow was in its death spiral of prompt critical.

The next event would stop the runaway nuclear reaction dead in its tracts. The pressurized sub cooled water in the entire reactor vessel suddenly flashed to superheated steam and the nuclear reactions immediately shutdown which, as designed, prevented an extremely powerful nuclear explosion. However, the reactor death spiral continued. Without circulating cooling water, the uranium metal fuel assemblies in the reactor core began to rapidly melt from decay heat. The corrosive chemical reaction of the melting fuel assemblies mixed with the superheated steam separated the compound hydrogen from oxygen (H2O) releasing hundreds of metric tons of explosive hydrogen gas into the reactor vessel. The vessel now contained a flaming molten core. Deadly alpha, beta and high energy gamma radiation waves filled the reactor compartment as the molten uranium core quickly melted and breached the reactor containment vessel walls.

Within seconds the hydrogen gas exploded with the force of hundreds of tons of TNT. The reactor vessel was blown apart and thrown through the bulkheads of the reactor compartment. The explosion ruptured the entire hull of the submarine throwing the Soviet DSRV off the back of *(Redacted)* and hurling it to the surface. The DSRV bobbed like a cork in the water alongside a plume of water reaching high into the air. The remnants of the submarine hull and equipment inside *(Redacted)* were scattered along the sea bottom like a mud-covered carpet of brightly glowing radioactive material lying beneath a dark and rocky landscape.

For the crewmember inside (*Redacted*) these events seemed to happen at the speed of light then milliseconds before slowing down even further as if in slow motion until time, with no further meaning, stood still and silent. After what could be described as an instantaneous eternity, the silence was suddenly broken by a blast of noise… followed by a gust of air… a wall of green and then darkness… nothing but warm peaceful darkness. Through the labyrinth of darkness flashes of light spiraled past becoming faster and faster and then stopped with a crack as suddenly as it began.

The sun reflected off the small white rocks along the blacktop road. An occasionally small seashell added a variety of color to the surroundings.

The spirit of USS *(Redacted)* (SSN-*Hull Number Classified*) now with its entire crew onboard rose from the ocean depths… on Eternal Patrol.

In Memoriam

Eternal Father, Strong to Save
(The Navy Hymn)

Eternal Father, strong to save,
Whose arm hath bound the restless wave,
Who bidd'st the mighty ocean deep
Its own appointed limits keep;
Oh, hear us when we cry to Thee,
For those in peril on the sea!

O Christ! Whose voice the waters heard
And hushed their raging at Thy word,
Who walkedst on the foaming deep,
And calm amidst its rage didst sleep;
Oh, hear us when we cry to Thee,
For those in peril on the sea!

Epilogue

As described, the nuclear attack submarine USS *(Redacted)* (SSN-**Hull Number Classified Secret**) collided with a submerged mountain in the Atlantic in an area south of the Azores in January 1968. More recently in 2005, the nuclear attack submarine USS *San Francisco* (SSN-711) also collided with a submerged mountain. On January 8, 2005, the USS *San Francisco* was approximately 360 miles southeast of Guam in the Pacific, traveling at a speed in excess of 30 knots. The navigational charts used by the ship's crew did not show the submerged mountain, protruding up from the ocean floor. The *San Francisco* smashed into it head-on. The incredible thing about this incident: despite running into a rock-solid object at more than 30 miles an hour, at a depth of 525 feet, the San Francisco did not sink, nor did it experience a reactor shutdown. The USS *San Francisco's* crew members were thrown about, in some cases, over distances in excess of 20 feet. The majority of the 137 members of the crew suffered some type of injury. One crewmember later passed due to his injuries. Further inspection of the boat later demonstrated what happened. As with *(Redacted)*, the submarine's bow compartment was crushed inward when the USS *San Francisco* ran into the submerged mountain. Incredibly, the submarine was able to transit under its own power back to port on Guam. The survival of the USS *San Francisco* and its crew is directly attributable to safety measures taken by U.S. Navy decades earlier following the loss of the USS *Thresher* in 1963. The excellent training of the *San Francisco* crew should also not be discounted. Unlike those onboard *(Redacted)* who tragically perished, fate played a more favorable role and indeed saved the USS *San Francisco* as well as the lives of the brave crew onboard.

Author Biography

Bio: Lieutenant USN (Ret) Tom Gaston served aboard five submarines from 1956 until his retirement in 1976. He rose from the enlisted ranks and received his commission as Ensign from Officer Candidate School in Newport, RI after graduation from the University of Texas in Austin in 1965. His undergraduate degree is in Applied Mathematics and received his master's degree in Finance from SIUE and the Citadel in 1976. He earned both his Silver Dolphins as enlisted and Gold Dolphins as a commissioned officer. Following his career in the Navy, he joined the Nuclear Engineering Department of Ohio Edison Company in Akron, Ohio as an Economic Analyst and Nuclear Fuel Planner. In 1995, as Owner/President, he established his own consulting company Nuclear Fuels Management Services, Inc. He developed nuclear power plant fuel planning and procurement strategies for public utility companies. His publications include *"Report on Analysis of Optimum Uranium Raw Material Inventory Levels,"* presented at the NEI Conference in Williamsburg, Virginia in 1995. He was employed as a Principal Nuclear Fuel Consultant at FirstEnergy Corporation in Akron, Ohio from 2006 until his retirement in 2009. He currently resides with his wife Bonnie in Rapid City, South Dakota.